Ted van Lieshout

Ted van Lieshout, a leading poet and author in The Netherlands, was born in Eindhoven in 1955 and now lives in Amsterdam. After graduating from the Rietveld Academy, where he studied illustration and graphic design, he worked for various publishers, designing book covers and making illustrations for newspapers and magazines. In 1982 he started illustrating for *De blauw geruite kiel*, a then famous literary magazine for children, and he published his first poetry and stories in it two years later. In 1986, his first book, *Raafs Reizend Theater (Raven's Travelling Theatre)* and a volume of children's poetry, *Van verdriet kun je grappige hoedjes vouwen (You Can Fold Sorrow into Funny Hats)*, were published. Both books were followed by a rapid succession of award-winning prose and poetry for children, as well as plays for theatre and television. His tories and   ed by a elancholy   nated by e search f

Ted van Lieshout

brothers

Translated by Lance Salway

An imprint of HarperCollins*Publishers*

For more information about the author
and his work, visit his website at:
www.tedvanlieshout.myweb.nl

First published in The Netherlands by Van Goor in 1996 as Gebr.
First published in Great Britain by CollinsFlamingo in 2001

CollinsFlamingo is an imprint of
HarperCollins*Publishers* Ltd,
77-85 Fulham Palace Road, Hammersmith,
London W6 8JB

The HarperCollins website address is
www.**fire**and**water**.com

ISBN 978-0-00-711231-9

For Carla, Harry and Albert

Eindhoven
Sunday 4 March 1973

Afternoon

Cheers, Maus,

This isn't the beginning. It's the end of your diary. I sneaked into your room and searched through the drawers in your desk until I found it. I smuggled the diary out, opened it, and leafed through it until I came to the first blank page, and now I've started to write. No, I haven't read what *you've* written. Really I haven't. Honestly not. There's probably a law against reading someone else's diary without permission. Maybe there's also a law against *writing* in someone else's diary, but I'm doing it anyway.

The carnival began today. No, this isn't a mistake, though I can just hear you saying, 'That can't be right, surely. It's only September.'

But it *is* right, Maus, because you've been dead six months now. One hundred and eighty-one days have gone by without you. It's your birthday tomorrow, but you're not here, so there's nothing to celebrate. You would have been fifteen, but time stood still for you at fourteen. And I'm not fifteen any more. My birthday was at the end of January as usual. If all goes well, I'll be seventeen next year, and then eighteen and nineteen; time is pushing us further and further apart and there's nothing anyone can do about it.

I expect you'll want to know why I'm writing in your diary. Haven't I got anything better to do? No, Maus, I haven't got anything better to do. You surely don't think I'm going to the carnival when I don't need to any more?

Today, when we were having lunch, Mum casually announced that she was going to get rid of you: 'Oh, by the way, Luke, I'm going to clear out Marius's room tomorrow, so if there's anything of his that you want, then you'd better take it today.'

'Why?' I asked, pretending not to know what she meant. 'There's no rubbish in there.'

'You know perfectly well what I mean. I'm going to clear out his things.'

'You mean you're going to put them in boxes and store them in the cellar?'

'No, I mean that I'm going to burn them in the back garden tomorrow.'

I thought Mum was joking at first, so I said, 'Good idea, it'll be fun to have a bonfire.' But then I realised from the serious look on her face that she meant it.

'Why?' I asked again.

'Because that's the way I want to say goodbye to him,' she said. 'If you want to keep anything of your brother's then of course you can. But I must ask you to keep it in your own room and not leave it lying around.'

'Are you really going to burn *everything*?' I could hardly believe my ears.

'I'm going to put every single thing on the bonfire and then I'm going to sit down on a chair and watch.'

'Sounds pretty gloomy.'

'Don't worry, it won't upset me,' said Mum. 'It's Marius's birthday tomorrow. So I want to make a special day of it.'

'Some birthday present!' I said angrily. 'Setting fire to all his things like that! If you get rid of everything then it'll feel as though Marius never existed.'

'I don't need his things to remind me of him every day.'

'I still think you should leave his room as it is. At least you can go in there and sit down and look around.'

'I'm not going to have a shrine in my house,' said Mum. 'I'm going to turn it into an ironing room. Then we'll be able to get all that junk out of the bathroom at long last.' She spread a dollop of butter on her roll, then scraped off the excess and pushed it behind the rim of the butter dish. You should have seen Dad's face, but he didn't say a word. He made a great show of producing a clean handkerchief, shaking it open, and wiping the mixture of butter and breadcrumbs from the dish. Then he carefully folded his handkerchief round the gunge and calmly put the bundle back in the pocket of his Sunday suit. You should have seen Mum's face, but she didn't say anything.

She cut some extra slices of cheese and covered her roll with them, even though she knew perfectly well that Dad swore by the old saying that cheese on butter is food for the devil.

With her mouth full of roll and butter and cheese, Mum said, 'Anyway, it was six months ago now. It's time to move on.' She was getting impatient and it was beginning to show, Maus: she gulped down the last of her roll, put on a stern expression, and briskly brushed imaginary crumbs from the table. 'We could talk about this for hours, Luke, but my mind is made up. Parting with his possessions is my way of saying goodbye.'

'And what about *my* way?' I asked.

'What *is* your way?'

I shrugged my shoulders, because I'd never thought about it; I didn't know I was supposed to have one. And of course she immediately seized the opportunity to kick the ground lovingly from under my feet.

'Well, that's up to you to decide. But first have a look and see if you want anything of your brother's. As far as I'm concerned you can take the whole lot into your own room. Just stay away from his desk, that's all; keep out of his private things.'

'Dad, do you understand any of this?' I asked. 'What do you think about it?'

'Leave me out of this, please,' Dad said with a wave of his hand. 'I'm not going to take sides. I can quite see why your mother wants to let go of Marius with a grand gesture. But wanting to keep his things has its own logic too.'

I asked Dad what he would do.

'I think we should put everything in boxes,' he said, 'but I know for sure that I'd never look inside them again. Your mother's idea of setting fire to Marius's things has something of a ritual about it and that appeals to me.'

'I'll be sending them up after him, in smoke,' Mum explained.

'My mother the Indian sending smoke signals,' I said.

'You can mock as much as you like, Luke, I couldn't care less. I knew you wouldn't understand.'

'I understand perfectly well and I think it's a nice gesture, but you don't believe in heaven so what's the point of sending Marius's things up after him?'

'I don't know for certain that heaven doesn't exist.'

'And I,' said Dad, putting on his solemn old man's voice, 'I am of the firm belief that if there is a God, then Heaven really does exist.'

Mum and I stared at our plates in silence for a moment or two – we never go to church and Dad always gets very annoyed about it.

'Yes, yes, I know I'm an old bore,' Dad said with a deep sigh, pushing his plate aside. 'You've told me that often enough. So carry on with your arguing, only just leave me out of it, that's all.' He took a fat cigar from his breast-pocket and held it up to his ear and listened as he rolled it between his fingers. Yes, Maus, it sounded OK, we could tell that from his face. Dad took his cigar cutter, snipped off the end of the cigar and lit it with his silver lighter. Then he sat back in his chair and smoked, staring into space.

Of course I wasn't at all put out by Dad's familiar stunt with the cigar that said: even though you may be able see me, I'm not really here. I turned back to Mum: 'So you're going to get rid of everything with one grand gesture. For good and all. If you clear out Marius's room, it'll be almost like murder!'

'Do stop showing off, Luke,' Mum said loftily. 'You're dancing the dying swan again.'

'He gets that melodramatic streak from you,' Dad said unexpectedly.

'Nonsense, those histrionics come straight from your side of the family.'

'How do you work that out?' demanded Dad. '*You're* the one who's taken it into her head to light a bonfire in the back garden. I come from a long line of poor farmers who spent all day up to their ankles in mud.' We come from very humble beginnings, you see, and have travelled a very long way to reach this house with room for at least ten families. We'd heard it all before.

'The soil is sandy here, so all that stuff about mud is nonsense, for a start,' said Mum, who wasn't taken in either.

'It used to rain a lot,' grinned Dad. 'For seven weeks on end sometimes. Even the cows had to swim.'

'It's never ever rained here for seven weeks on end, my sweet!'

'You don't know what you're talking about, my darling. Long before you were born, I was paddling about in waders from early morning till late at night, tipping buckets of water out of the Kempen.'

'Oh yes?' said Mum scornfully. 'That was when Brabant was still a polder, I suppose.'

'I'm leaving the table,' I warned. 'If you two can't be serious about this, then I've got better things to do.'

'What were we talking about again?' asked Mum, rummaging for her packet of cigarettes.

'You want to put Marius on a funeral pyre. *That's* what we were talking about!'

So now you know, Maus, we're not descended from gypsies, like Mum used to tell us, but from Indians. We never liked playing cowboys and Indians when we were small because we always stuck up for the Indians. Now we know why. And tomorrow an Indian fire is to be lit in your honour. Here in our own back garden.

Look down through the clouds, if you can, and you'll see far below a tiny squaw with bleached blonde hair sending smoke signals into the air. Read the messages in the round grey puffs. If all goes well, you'll be able to decipher the following words: *here-are-the-things-that-you-left-behind*.

Try to get a look at the squaw's face. It's our mum. Behind her is our dad, wearing clogs. You'll see that they're standing in our garden, behind our house, in our road, in our town, in our country, in our continent, on our planet, in our universe. Your mother is tossing memories onto a smouldering fire, one by one.

I have to admit that Mum has thought up a fine way of saying goodbye to you in — how shall I put it? — a definitive manner. She's setting you free; life must go on.

Wouldn't it be wonderful if heaven really *did* exist and we could send smoke signals up to you? If we could talk to each other again in little clouds of smoke? But you didn't believe in heaven.

'If you ask someone at eight o'clock in the morning where heaven is, they'll point upwards,' you said once. 'Ask them again at eight o'clock in the evening and they'll point upwards again, even though the earth has turned a good half revolution and they're pointing in exactly the opposite direction. So they really don't know and they're just pointing at random.'

'Perhaps heaven is all around?' I suggested.

'Then in that case it would have to be way past Pluto and that's too far,' you said. 'Because if God created us in His own image, then He can't see past the end of His own nose, either.'

When Mum said that she was going to burn *all* your things, I immediately thought about the diary that I gave you two years ago on your thirteenth birthday. I thought, is she going to burn that, too? I deliberately haven't asked her because I don't know if she's remembered that this diary exists. With any luck she's forgotten all about it. I'd really hate it if she threw it into the flames. It would seem as though she was burning your thoughts, too, and what would be the point of that?

That's why I've quietly stolen the diary from your desk. Stolen, because Mum made a point of saying that I must keep away from your private things. But I did it all the same because this is what I've decided: I am going to write in your diary so that my thoughts will be there as well. If Mum remembers your diary and tries to burn it, I'll be able to stop her because she will be burning *my* written thoughts too! It's as simple as that.

So you see, Maus, I'm not sitting here with my nose buried in your diary because I'm curious to see what you've written in it (though I am, of course). By writing in your diary I can save it, and that way something of you will continue to exist.

The only trouble is I've no idea what to write next. Or have I already written enough?

Evening

Dear Maus,

I felt very superior at supper, because Dad and Mum were all dressed up for the carnival party at the bowling alley, and were sitting there looking really stupid. Boring as ever, Dad was wearing his peasant smock, but then I suppose any old bloke of sixty-five, with a red handkerchief round his neck with the ends pulled through a matchbox cover would look pretty stupid. Mum was wearing a little something she'd run up out of an old evening dress. She said that what she was dressed as was 'art', but her costume had a neckline halfway to her navel and the hem was about the same height as her fanny. Oh well, art or tart, it doesn't really matter much at carnival time. And I have to admit, she's got really good legs for a woman in her late thirties.

I must say I was really rather pleased with my little scheme to save your diary, and I thought that I'd actually written enough in it this afternoon. But I couldn't leave it at that, could I? I just had to draw Mum's attention to the fact that she can't burn your diary now because it contains my personal thoughts as well.

The reaction was very disappointing. Instead of giving a cheer and applauding the remarkable ingenuity of their flesh and blood, Mum and Dad were furious and didn't believe me when I said that, although I'd written in the diary, I hadn't read any of it.

'Anyway,' I said calmly, 'you won't be able to burn the diary now.'

'You'll have to get up earlier than that if you want to get the better of me,' said Mum. She crossed one bare leg over the other, and I was irritated to see that she was still playing the role of mother, despite looking as she did. 'All I have to do is tear your pages out of the diary and throw the rest of it on the fire.'

I had no answer to that and I sat in stubborn silence for the rest of the meal. Mum can't stand this, as you know, but keeping my mouth shut is the only weapon I have when I don't get my own way.

So here I am with your diary again, because my plan now is to write so much in it that the diary becomes more mine than yours. Then if that rotten cow tears out my pages, she'll have to destroy the whole thing, and I don't think she's up to that.

Of course it must seem strange for me to be writing in your diary and talking to you as if you'll be able to read it one day. But I'm not as stupid as all that. You're dead and, like all the other dead people who've been buried, you're turning into a skeleton (if you haven't already). I've often tried to picture you decomposing in that dark box under the ground, dressed in your favourite clothes. How long does it take for the body of a dead person to become a skeleton? Is it weeks? Months? Years? What stage are you at now? Do you actually *know* that you're dead and buried? Did you notice it happening?

It took place six months ago precisely. It was Monday, 4th September 1972, and it was still summer. I came home and Mum was waiting for me with a tear-stained face.

'I've got something really dreadful to tell you,' she said, and I could see that she was searching desperately for words. She crossed her arms over her chest and hugged her shoulders. I knew that she was doing this because she didn't want to be touched. She looked at me as though she was hoping that I would guess what she was going to say, but I wanted to hear it from her own lips. She looked away from me and said quietly, 'Marius died in hospital this afternoon.'

I don't know how it feels when you die, but I can certainly tell you how it feels when you hear that someone who was always there has ceased to exist. An electric tingling started in my stomach and flashed up to my head in one second flat. It was as if my insides had instantly frozen up, and yet, funnily enough, it felt as though they were burning too. It was like the feeling you get when you put your half-frozen hands near a heater, but this was happening inside instead.

I can't remember now what I said. I only know that it wasn't: *That's dreadful, but it could have been much worse, so it's turned out rather well.* That's the sort of thing that Mum always says. But it *couldn't* have been any worse. Perhaps I didn't say anything at all. Mum was crying and I didn't want to see her tears. I bolted out of the kitchen, up the stairs and hid behind the door of my room.

I sat there and cried very quietly, until I had to catch my breath. I was in tears for ten minutes, or maybe a quarter of an hour. After that I washed my face in cold water and stared at myself in the mirror for a while. I don't know why I did that. Perhaps I thought that I might look different now that I didn't have a brother any more. But it wasn't so.

By the evening my eyes were no longer red, but Mum's face was still puffy and her eyes were runny from crying. She waited till Gran arrived and then she shut herself away in the big bedroom. Gran and I sat in the living room all on our own, because Dad had made himself scarce and was now inaccessible in his office – which was what the study has been called ever since he retired. We could only tell he was at home at all by the strong smell of cigar smoke escaping through the crack under the door.

When Dad came out to go to the loo, I had a quick look to see what he was doing. An open folder was lying on his desk, next to three ashtrays full of cigar butts. At the top of the page was written *Last Will and Testament*. The text had been crossed through with a slanting line. I was scared that Dad would catch me, so I only had time to read what he had written at the side in bold writing: 'Never, ever crossed my mind that I should survive one of my own children.'

I went quickly back to the living room. I felt deeply ashamed because I'd realised for the first time that I was now the sole heir. I felt like a greedy bastard.

In those American series on TV, people are always falling into each other's arms whenever anything (or nothing) terrible happens. It wasn't like that with us. Dad, Mum and I, all three of us, wanted to be apart in one way or another. Each of us cut ourselves off from the others and chose our own place. We didn't want support from each other. It was as if a big sharp knife had cut off our air supply and we needed to find space to gulp fresh air. I think that we were all searching for an answer to one question: now that Marius was gone, how were we going to carry on living without him? Because the strange thing was that although life seemed to have stopped for us, it was still going on. The earth was still turning and the sun hadn't switched off. But the world certainly came to an end on the day you died, or at least the world as you knew it.

Gran cooked something, but Dad and Mum wouldn't come and eat. And Gran herself said that she'd sampled so much while she was cooking that she'd lost her appetite. Since that would have meant that she'd done all that cooking for nothing, I managed to force something down, much against my will.

I spent the whole evening running up and down stairs, listening at the doors to the rooms where Dad and Mum had tucked themselves away; I was feeling a bit worried because now that you'd died, the rest of us might just as easily drop dead too.

Gran and I also had to stay by the telephone and the front door, to fob off all those people who wanted to tell us how terrible it was, as if we didn't already know. When the envelopes for the funeral cards arrived, we wrote addresses and licked stamps.

At one point, Mum came out of her room to fetch an old bottle of red wine from Dad's wine cellar. I saw from the label that it was bottled in 1958, the year you were born.

Gran asked, 'Wouldn't you like a glass with that, dear?'

'No, I'm going to drink straight from the bottle, even if it did cost five hundred guilders,' Mum said. 'I'm going to knock it back and sit and watch TV.'

Mum stood there in her long blue nightdress (you know, the one that's so embarrassing because you can see her nipples) and she reminded me of the Statue of Liberty in New York. Her right hand was clutching the neck of the bottle as if it was a torch and it looked as though she was going to raise it proudly in the air at any minute.

'Does Dad know about that?' I pointed to the dusty bottle.

'I don't need his permission,' she said, 'and besides, I'm not going to tell him.'

'Are you going to get drunk?' I asked, as Gran trotted to the front door yet again.

'You don't get drunk on a five hundred guilder bottle of wine, darling, just a bit tipsy.'

'Why don't you just come and sit down here with us?'

'Because I want to get sloshed all by myself and feel miserable.'

'I'm feeling miserable too.'

What Mum said then really got up my nose because she tried to tell me there were different degrees of grief: 'Yes, I know you're grieving too, of course, but my grief is greater than yours because today I lost my son.'

'I've lost my brother so my grief is just as great as yours,' I said.

'The grief of a mother is greater than the grief of a brother.'

'I don't see why!' I blurted out. 'You're still someone's mother, but I'm no one's brother any more.'

Mum was taken aback for a moment but you know

what she's like: 'Even so, it's still worse for a mother than it is for a brother. I'm his mother and I gave birth to him. And besides, I knew him longer than you did.'

'We each knew him for the same length of time,' I said.

'You can't remember anything about when you were very little. You were only thirteen months old when Marius was born.' A faint smile appeared on her face and I could tell that she thought she'd had the last word.

'You didn't know Marius most of your life but I've never had a life where he didn't exist,' I said with deadly seriousness, because it was very important to me.

'Oh, darling, won't you please stop this nonsense? My head just can't take any more. I only came downstairs for this bottle.' Mum turned her back on me very firmly, lifted her nightdress so as not to trip over the hem, and shuffled out of the room.

I wanted to shout something after her but I kept quiet because Gran had come back into the room. She always had an immediate attack of nerves whenever she heard Mum and me bickering. (Gran really flew off the handle not so long ago. She said: 'You're both as bad as each other: a fishwife and a foghorn!' We laughed with relief because it sounded so comical coming from her.)

Mum made a great drama out of her grief but Dad kept his buttoned up. A day or two later, when I took some old newspapers into the garage, I came upon Dad howling in a corner. He was so angry at being caught that he pushed me out of the garage, his arms flailing wildly. I was cross at first but then I went away quietly and said nothing about it. No one is supposed to know that fathers can cry.

Then they put your body in a coffin and buried that coffin in the cemetery. They gave you a flat, grey, shiny marble stone. IN GRATITUDE FOR HIS LIFE is written on it. Mum thought that up. In the middle there's a big MARIUS, and under that MARINUS THOMAS in smaller letters with our surname, and after that the facts: 5 MARCH 1958 – 4 SEPTEMBER 1972.

Your grave is the sixteenth one in the row. The graves on either side of you have got tombstones too, so I can at least tell you that you'll have elderly neighbours from now on. One is Petronella Rademaker and she was ninety, the other is Johannes van Aalst and he was eighty-four. So you see, Maus, you aren't the first person in the world to die and you won't be the last.

As I walked past the gravestones in your row, peering curiously at the ages, I realised that just about all the people lying there were old. I felt a sudden stab of pain inside. One boy of fourteen lying beside all those old people. What on earth is he doing there among all the old dears? I added up all the ages and divided by the number of dead people, and Maus, how's this for a nice surprise: you average out at sixty-nine years old!

Do you think that's a mean thing to say? It's all your mother's fault, really. She impressed upon us from an early age that everything is relative. Whenever I cut my knee open and ran crying to her, the answer was always, 'Yes, Luke, I know it's awful but it would be far worse to have a leg off.' And when, much against your will, you had to wear glasses because of your migraine, she said: 'Losing an eye would be much worse.'

Do you remember the time when we were about seven years old and Mum sent us to pick cherries for bottling? I was up in the tree and you were on a ladder propped against it. The cherries were so shiny and red that we didn't just hang them over our ears, we ate them too. We didn't stop to think that they were morello cherries for brandy.

Then we asked each other why Mum had sent us to pick sour cherries when she knew perfectly well that we'd eat them and get stomach ache. We decided that it was high time we found out if she really loved us.

Together we climbed down and went to find her. Then we asked the question that we'd thought up: 'Mum, if there was a fire in the middle of the night and you had to jump out of the window, what's the first thing you would take with you?'

'That all depends,' Mum said. 'Am I in bed on my own or is Dad with me?'

We looked at each other, because we couldn't see what this had got to do with it.

'Couldn't you just give us an answer?'

'Well now,' said Mum. 'If Dad is beside me and there's a fire, then I'd swing him round by the ankles to break the window, then drop him on the floor and jump into the firemen's safety net with the two of you in my arms.'

Dad laughed at that and we didn't understand why.

'But if Dad isn't beside me,' Mum went on, 'then I'd grab the two of you by the ankles, smash the window, drop you on the floor and jump into the safety net by myself. Does that answer your question?'

'I suppose so,' we said doubtfully, and left the room to compare notes. We came to the conclusion that Mum loved herself the best, then us, and Dad least of all. It was dreadful to think that she didn't love us the best, but it would have been worse if she had loved Dad more than us, so we couldn't complain. It was dreadful but it could have been even worse, so on the whole it had turned out rather well.

When you died, Maus, none of us could think of anything worse. There's nothing relative about death. Mum didn't say: 'It's awful that Marius has died but luckily I've got another son, so I'm still a mother.'

A man who loses his wife is called a widower, a woman who loses her husband is a widow, and children without parents are orphans. But what do you call a brother who doesn't have a brother (or sister) any more? There isn't a name for it. And anyway, I wouldn't know how to look it up. Can you still be someone's brother if that someone no longer exists?

But it doesn't really matter any more. A mother has to mother, a father has to father, and a brother has to brother. And as there's nothing left to brother, I can't be a brother now. I wasn't a very good brother anyway. I was a useless brother: I often left you on your own even though I knew you hated it. But I really would like to find out whether I'm still a brother now that you're no longer here. What do you think? Or don't you care any more?

Evening

Dear Maus,

I've brought my pen and your diary and I'm now sitting in your room, because I've suddenly realised that I won't be able to do this any more after this evening.

I sat down at your desk very carefully. I was a bit scared, in case everything here (your bed, your desk, your chair, the books on the shelf, the photos and maps on the walls) should suddenly spring to life and attack me: 'You're in forbidden territory! Get out! Go back to your own room!' Still, this would only be fair, considering that I almost always told you to get lost if you came into my room uninvited. During the past few days I've thought a lot about one of those times.

It was in 1970, because that's the date on the back of the drawing I was working on when you came into my room. You know the one I mean, that drawing of a tree you said you wanted to have for your birthday. I wouldn't even consider it because I thought it was pretty good myself. I

said: 'You can't have it, but I'll leave it to you when I die.'
But I gave it to you later anyway.

I was still working on it that day, so of course I couldn't
let you see it; I never allow anyone to see a drawing until
it's finished. I shielded the paper with my arms and
snapped at you so that you'd know you weren't welcome:
'What do you want?'

'Nothing,' you said. 'I've just come to see you.'

'I'm busy.'

'What with?'

'I'm drawing.'

'Oh yes? You're probably tracing something again,' you
teased, and sat down on my bed. That really got up my
nose because my bed isn't a place where other people can
just park their bums, so I said, 'Why don't you go and
annoy someone else?'

'I'm not doing anything, am I? I'm just sitting here.'

'And I can't stand it because you're sitting there
watching my fingers. Why don't you go away and do
something?'

'Like what?'

'Go and read a book or, I don't know, go and play with
yourself.'

'Oh, you mean I'm disturbing you because *you* want to
play with yourself? Why didn't you say so?'

'I want to play with myself. OK?'

'I've gone already.'

'Good.'

'You're a real prick, d'you know that?'

You were nearly out of the door when I said: 'Sorry, Maus, but I really *am* busy now. But it was nice of you to come.' Yes, I was as two-faced as that and you saw through me right away.

'How come you're only nice to me when I'm leaving?'

'It's not your fault. I just want to be alone, that's all.'

'And I don't, but a fat lot you care.'

You're right, Maus, I didn't really care. But how was I to know you were going to die? I felt really sorry afterwards about the things I couldn't change any more. Like getting angry when you had to go to the loo just when it was our turn to do the washing up, just to give one example. I had a lot of regrets, especially in the beginning.

I'm sure that other brothers behave towards each other just like we did. The only difference is that those brothers are still alive, and we aren't any more. I mean, of course, *you* aren't alive any more, but I am.

It's as if your room is waiting quietly for you to open the door and come in, so that everything, so that life can go on once more. Your room has been waiting such a long time, all for nothing.

I don't really know your room very well. When you were still alive I hardly ever came in here. (I have been in here during the past six months, but mainly to look something up in one of your atlases or to borrow a record.) Even so I can see that nothing has changed. The walls are still covered with photos from the *Music Express* and, most of all, masses of maps, old and new.

I can't remember exactly when you started that craze; Alex was still living just down the road when he infected you with the atlas virus. Then you suddenly announced that you wanted to be an explorer, even though everything has been discovered already, as you could easily tell from the maps. How often did I see you and Alex lying together on the floor, tracing round-the-world journeys in the open atlas with your fingers?

All those maps will be going on the fire tomorrow. They were so very important to you, but your mother's going to set fire to the whole bang lot. Along with all the other things you collected. They've lost their value now that you're dead.

To be honest, I don't think I'd find it easy to decide which of your things to keep. I've already got the best thing of all. It's a memory of a time when you were twelve. This one: Mum and I were sitting on the sofa in front of the television watching a documentary about Indonesia. You took the big atlas from the bookcase, lay down cosily on the floor at our feet and turned to the map of South-East Asia. You couldn't have cared less about the images on the telly, but those on a 1:13500000 map showing two millimetres of water lying between Sumatra and Java – now they *were* interesting. And you chattered away: 'Mum, why is Malaysia in two parts that are so far away from each other, and why is one part stuck onto Borneo? And logically, the other part should belong to Indonesia, even though it wouldn't all be islands then. And what is Singapore exactly? Who does it belong to? Is it a city or a country or both? And why haven't they dug a Panama Canal in that narrow peninsula between Burma and the Straits of Malacca? They've got to sail all the way round now.'

'We're watching the telly,' said Mum.

'Do *you* know, Luke?'

'The Panama Canal is in Central America.'

'I know that, idiot. I mean a canal *like* the Panama Canal.'

'Never mind about that now,' said Mum, 'We're watching the television. Look at that, isn't Borobudur beautiful? Do come and have a look.'

But you didn't look, because you'd made yet another discovery.

'Hey, Mum, look at this island I've found in the Gulf of Thailand. I wonder if it belongs to the United Nations. Guess what its name is?' And you said a very dirty word that means vagina.

It was just your luck to get away without being punished for saying out loud a word that was forbidden in our house under any circumstances. How we laughed when we asked

Dad – our dad! – whether we could go on holiday there. Wasn't it wonderful when we explained to him, the man who claimed to know everything, that the place wasn't a swearword but a small island that really did exist? Even Mum couldn't help joining in our laughter then.

I need such memories, Maus. I need those anecdotes that are repeated so often that they take root inside your head. You'd be amazed if you knew how much of you I'm already beginning to forget. At first I thought that I was forgetting you on purpose, because it might make it easier for me to get used to the idea that you aren't here any more. But it isn't deliberate. It's accidental. I noticed this the other day. I was trying to remember what your voice sounded like and I couldn't find it anywhere in my head. Not a sausage. Gone. Vanished. I began to panic because I wanted so much to remember. I couldn't understand why I could remember your face but not your voice.

The answer is obvious really. If I try to recall you in my mind, I can only see you hazily in the shadows of the house. I don't see your face, just sometimes your hand or foot (it's always the foot with the scar where the iron fell on it). If I want to see your face clearly, I need a photo to remind me. One of the photos from the album. Only then can I see you distinctly. And as there isn't a photograph of your voice, not even a tape recording, I have nothing to cling on to. Do you see what I mean? Forgetting happens by accident.

That's why it's important to keep as many of your things as possible. They help me to see you more clearly, they help me to remember that you once had a life in which you were happy. And that's another reason why your diary must survive. If Mum burns everything, *everything*, and then someone comes along and claims that you never existed, then I'll have the proof that you really did live and think.

I jerked open the door of your cupboard with such force that your clothes swung in the draught. A couple of empty coathangers clashed together in fright.

I looked at your clothes, shook my head, and thought to myself, what a pity, the boy who wore those has worn out. I felt this was rather a nice thought. Then I had a crazy idea – well, perhaps not as crazy as all that when you remember that it's carnival time and everyone is dressing up. I decided to celebrate my own private carnival.

I got undressed and put on your clothes – your threadbare jeans, because it's easy to tell from those that the boy who wore them has worn out, and your blue sweater with the holes at the elbows.

You'd think that brothers who are only thirteen months apart would fit into each other's clothes. Not us. When you were thirteen, you shot up like a bamboo shoot, while I just didn't seem to want to grow. Now I'm sixteen and you've stayed at fourteen, but even so your elbows and your knees are too long on me. I had to turn up the legs of your jeans at least twice before my feet came into sight. I could fasten the belt easily but the zip won't close because, "with your body on", my bum is much too big (or maybe my dick's too big, that might be the reason). The clothes are too tight at my shoulders and thighs as well. You're hugging me, Maus. Isn't that wonderful? I'm wearing you. I'm spending this carnival dressed as my brother.

Your record-player is in its usual place. I hardly dared switch it on because everything in your room has been silent for so long. But when I turned the knob, the little light came on and the turntable began to move as usual.

I looked through your pile of LPs to see if there were any I wanted to keep. Aha, there was *Clouds* by Joni Mitchell. I took the record out of the sleeve and put it on the turntable. Once again, after such a long time, your room is filled with music.

If you receive Mum's smoke signals tomorrow and this LP isn't with them, then you'll know that you've lent it to me forever:

> *There's a sorrow in his eyes*
> *Like the angel made of tin*
> *What will happen if I try*
> *To place another heart in him*

Evening

Dear Maus,

I'm back in my own room now. Actually, I suppose you could say that I was chased out of your room. I heard the sound of the front door and Mum and Dad's voices in the hall. They'd come back home after celebrating the carnival with a couple of drinks in the bar at the bowling alley, and I didn't want them to know that I'd been writing in your room.

I don't need to listen at the top of the stairs, Maus, because we both know what happens after they've been out for the evening. Our dad's gone down to the cellar to choose a nice bottle of wine. Our mum has inspected all the glasses for smudges and has given the cleanest ones just one more wipe. They're in the sitting room now, chatting. And I bet they're having Burgundy, with a cigarette and a cigar. And when those have been smoked, the lights will go out downstairs and they'll go up to their bedroom, where the brandy is waiting. Nothing has really been the same since you died, yet at the same time nothing seems to have changed at all.

I want Mum to know that I've filled up so many pages in the diary that it's now more mine than it is yours. She'll have to destroy it completely if she wants to remove me altogether.

My plan is to stroll casually into your room just as Mum comes up the stairs. She'll ask me what I'm doing and then I'll just happen to mention that I've won the battle for your diary.

If I'm honest, though, Mum and Dad coming home wasn't the only reason why I fled from your room. Five times in a row I heard the words coming from your loudspeakers: *What will happen if I try to place another heart in him.* And there I was standing in the middle of your room in your sweater and trousers, as if I was trying to cram my heart into your clothes, as if I was trying to *be* you. But I'm not you and I can never become you, either. I was just an intruder, forced to beat a hasty retreat. And yes, that feeling of guilt swept over me once again, because the thought that you're still only fourteen years old is sometimes so hard to take.

But at least it's not like it was in the beginning. Then I felt terribly guilty because you had died. Not because it was my fault but because a younger brother isn't supposed to die. The oldest has lived the longest and so should be the first to go. That's what happens in all the fairy tales. That's how it should be – the nasty eldest son must die so that the beautiful younger son can live happily ever after. But I refused point-blank to die just to make you a hero. You died and I simply let it happen. I stood there and watched.

I *know* it's stupid of me to feel guilty and I don't go around with my head bowed low in shame, but there's a question I've never dared put to Mum and Dad: would they have preferred it if I had been the one who died, instead of you? Stupid, isn't it?

I've still got your clothes on. Because it's so good to be hugged by you.

Evening

Dear Maus,

Mum and Dad are in their bedroom now, watching a Western on television.

When I heard Mum coming up the stairs, I opened my door and made a big show of walking towards your room.

'What are you doing?' Mum asked. 'Shouldn't you be going to bed?'

'I don't have to go to school tomorrow.'

'I know that, but surely you haven't forgotten you're going to see the eye specialist?'

'Of course I haven't forgotten,' I said.

'It really won't be as bad as you think, you know,' Mum said. She stroked my cheek with the back of her hand. She does this a lot and she means to be affectionate but she always forgets that the diamond in her ring scratches.

'What are you going to his room for?'

'I'm going to see if there's anything else I want to keep. Oh, by the way, I've written such a lot in the diary now that it's really more mine than it is Marius's. So there's no point in tearing my pages out. You'll only ruin the whole thing.'

She tilted her head, coyly, turned up the corners of her mouth and said archly: 'But darling, surely I can just tear out the few pages that your brother wrote? How many did you say there were?'

I rolled my eyes, as if to say oh-why-don't-you-go-to-hell. Then I went into your room and switched on the light. Mum followed me.

'All right, my boy,' she said calmly. 'I can tell that you think I've lost my marbles. But I just want you to know that I think you've pulled a disgusting stunt with that diary. I expressly told you not to go through the things on his desk and yet you still went ahead and did it.'

'And so?'

'His diary is private. You should leave it well alone.'

'I haven't read any of it.'

'That's not the point. How would you like it if I went through *your* diary?'

'What makes you think I've got a diary?' I asked suspiciously.

'Because you once shouted hysterically that you'd written the whole truth about me in your diary and that after we were dead, everyone would know what a rotten mother I'd been.'

'That's true,' I said calmly.

'But even a rotten mother has her uses sometimes,' said

Mum, with the sort of giggle that comes after a few glasses of wine. 'If I'd been a nice lovey-dovey mummy, I'd never even have made it into your diary! At least I'm giving you something to write about.' She turned to go to the door. Then she saw a framed drawing propped against the wall, and picked it up. It was the drawing of the tree that I did in 1970.

'Did you forget to take this to your room?'

'I gave that drawing to Marius so it doesn't belong to me. You can burn it tomorrow.'

'Don't be so silly,' said Mum. 'You'll need to take an entrance exam to get into art school, and it would be a shame if you couldn't show them this drawing.'

'I still don't want it any more,' I said.

Mum shrugged her shoulders. Then she put the drawing of the tree against the wall, face outwards, and crossed to the door. She put her hand on the doorknob and then turned round once again. 'Oh, just one more thing, sweetie.'

'Yes?'

'Are you expecting a visitor this evening?'

'No, why?'

'Because your flies are undone.'

I went as red as a beetroot but luckily Mum didn't notice because she was already out of the room. Then I turned the drawing to face the wall again, because I didn't want to see it any more.

Maus, how terrible would it be if I read what you've written? Very terrible / a bit terrible / not all that terrible / really good? You see, if I write on the pages that you've already filled up, between the lines and the words and in the margins and anywhere there's room, then Mum won't be able to separate your part of the diary from mine. And so I'll be able to save your diary, because it must survive. Everything else, the photos, the things on the wall, and your clothes, they just say that you were here, but not what you were like and what you thought and felt. Not in words, anyway. That's why Mum mustn't get her claws on this diary. It mustn't be lost just because she wants to protect your privacy after death. You'd like some part of you to stay on in the world, wouldn't you, Maus? But if I write between your lines, you do realise that I can't avoid reading what's there already? I haven't got permission to read what you've written but I'm going to do it anyway, even if there *is* a law against it. And I have to admit that I want to read it very much indeed.

Midnight

Happy birthday to you, happy birthday to you, happy birthday dear Maus, happy birthday to you. Many happy returns of the day, because Monday 5th March started just a few moments ago. You would have been fifteen now. I've put out the light and lit a couple of candles. For you, Maus. Even though we're not having a party, I've come on a visit anyway.

[FRIDAY, 5 MARCH 1971] *I'm thirteen today.*

One more time: many happy returns of the day, even if it is for a birthday two years ago.

The nicest thing I got – from Mum and Dad – is a very old map of the world, from when the world hadn't been completely discovered yet. It isn't a real old map, but a copy of one, so it isn't really worth all that much. But it's nice that Mum found it for me all the same.

You could sail the seas then and bump into the coast of America by accident – it wasn't really a 'discovery', because people were already living there, so it had been discovered a long time before.

Yes, the native Indians were there before Columbus. And we're descended from them.

I read somewhere that those people ended up there, long before, after walking from Russia to Alaska across the ice. But I've since seen on television that the world wasn't always the way it is now, and this means that people may have spread across the world in a very different way. The fact is that, at one time, all the continents were joined together in a lump and this single continent was called Pangaea – that's Greek and you pronounce it Pan-gay-a. It means something like earth-together.

It didn't have a name then, of course, because in the very beginning, millions of years ago, there weren't any people at all, or if there were any, then they didn't write their language down. Or if they did write something down, then it's been lost. Anyway, Western Europe wasn't by the sea but was joined up to America, and Britain wasn't an island yet. Then, one day, Pangaea broke up in pieces for some reason and in the course of time the continents drifted apart.

Just like us. We're drifting apart too, just like the continents of Pangaea. You'll stay fourteen forever but I've already drifted past sixteen, whether I like it or not.

So if people already existed then, the Neanderthals for instance, then it was a really good thing that they already lived where they did and just drifted apart from each other, and didn't have to walk for days on end to start another nation in a different part of the world. And the amazing thing is that the continents are still drifting! So one day, in the far distant future, they'll collide with each other again, but then everything will be the wrong way round, because what used to be the coast of Pangaea will be squashed together and heaped up into mountains, which is what happened when India collided with Asia and the Himalayas came into being. And what used to be a fracture line becomes a coastal area. East becomes west and west becomes east. Then Japan will become a high mountain between Asia and America. And then there'll be a big problem, because Japan is called the land of the rising sun, but how can it be called that when it isn't an island in the sea any longer but a sort of mound between Siberia and the Rocky Mountains? I think that the sun will rise somewhere else in future, though I can't think where.

Gran gave me a subscription to "Music Express", and I also got record tokens and a diary from Luke. I wonder what gave him that idea?

Um.

I never asked for a diary, and I've no intention of ever keeping a diary either.

Well, that doesn't come as any surprise, Maus. When I flipped through the diary I couldn't help noticing that you hadn't written all that much.

I think Luke wants me to concentrate on writing so that I don't think about the trembling in my little finger. The stupid thing is, though, that it's the little finger on my left hand that trembles, but I write with my right hand!

But a diary? I said: 'Oh, how nice, a diary!' but I'm really not going to start keeping one, because I don't like writing, so I'll just say what my birthday was like: we ate chicken and that's all, so I didn't need to keep wiping my fingers while I picked the bones, and I went to see a film with half my class. It was good and then it was all over. So, here endeth my diary.

Sorry it wasn't a very good present but I didn't give you the diary for the reason you supposed.

I remember that you and I were sitting at the table together, sometime around my birthday two years ago, when I first noticed that the little finger on your left hand was trembling. I asked you to stick your hands in the air and it looked very strange: nine fingers standing still and just one little finger shaking.

'Is it some kind of trick?' I asked. 'That finger looks really weird.'

'I can't help it,' you said. 'It does it all by itself.'

We called Mum and she asked, 'Why on earth is that finger shaking all on its own like that?'

'I don't know,' you said, 'but I think it's weird too.'

Still, what did it matter, one trembling finger? It didn't hurt and you weren't really bothered by it, it was just a minor inconvenience, that's all. I thought then that it was a lot of fuss about nothing, but Mum dragged you off to the doctor who said that it was nervous tension. There was no clue in your school report with its grades of eights and nines but, even so, that's when I thought that it might be a good idea if you had a diary, so that you could write about that tension. I've got a diary too, because I often have things to say even when I don't want to talk to anyone.

[TUESDAY, 12 OCTOBER 1971] I've got nothing to do.

Six months later! You didn't write anything at all between March and October. Sorry my present was such rubbish.

I've got nothing at all to do and I'm bored rigid. I've fallen downstairs and sprained my ankle.

Because your trembling got worse so very slowly, we didn't really notice it but, by October, your left hand was shaking like an old man's. Perhaps you lost your grip on the banister and stumbled.

I'm not supposed to stand on my foot and so I don't have to go to school. There's no one at home and I can hobble about really well, so I've been having a good nose round – well, I had to because no one here ever tells me anything. I'm suffering from a chronic shortage of information.

Very witty. You pinched that from Mum. At the moment she doesn't have a 'chronic shortage' of anything but she manages to find double meanings in the most ordinary expressions. If she's talking to someone, and another person joins in the conversation and says 'Do you mind if I butt in?' she makes a great show of crossing her legs and saying, 'Here? Right this minute? Can't you even wait until we're alone?' Yes, you may well laugh.

First of all I had a good look round my own room

How about this for another good laugh. Mum and Auntie Kees were in a café last weekend, having a friendly drink (or six) together, when Mum had to go to the toilet. While she was having a really good pee, she suddenly realised that she'd forgotten to lift the lid and the pee was streaming all over the toilet bowl. She tried to stop peeing as quickly as she could but her knickers were wet through and the floor was drenched. Mum pulled off her wet knickers, stuffed them in her bag, and rushed out, too upset to clean up the once pristine toilet. Auntie Kees was waiting outside, dying for a pee, and our mum said, 'Well, Kees, I'd try and hold it if I were you. The toilets here are really disgusting!'

Go on then, laugh! It's party time, remember! It's your birthday! And it's carnival too. They're celebrating your birthday out there without even realising it.

and I came across this stupid diary again.

All right, then.

I've now read what I've written and I was quite right to say that I didn't want a diary. When I read the words: 'I think that the sun will rise somewhere else in future', it seemed as if they'd been written by someone who'd lost their marbles, because it isn't possible for the sun to rise somewhere else. And I'm only sitting here writing this now because I'm scared that anyone who reads that sentence will think I really am mad unless I say that I didn't mean it like that. I don't really think that the sun will rise somewhere else!

It actually sounds rather beautiful: the sun that rises somewhere else.

Then I went and had a good nose round in Mum and Dad's bedroom. And there I found two interesting things. The first thing was a sex book in the wardrobe, very dirty, with at least twenty naked women with beautifully arranged hair, which wouldn't be possible if you'd just taken all your clothes off. And they had far too much make-up on too! And there were advertisements from people who wanted to do all sorts of dirty things with each other but "no fin.ben." I must try and find out what that means because it must be something really filthy if nobody wants to do it. And the second thing was one condom in a drawer of the bedside table, so our mum and dad actually do it. Or rather, they don't do it, because it was a condom that hadn't been used.

I know about that dirty book in the wardrobe and I didn't know what 'no fin.ben.' meant either. I thought it might have something to do with a Finnish sauna but then I suddenly worked it out. It means: no financial benefit. I was really disappointed about that.

After that I had a good look round Luke's room

Where you had no right to be!

and I found a very strange letter under the blotter on his desk.

Oh no, not that. Not again. Let's stay friends on this special day.

It's the rough draft of a letter to Mum and Dad. I read it and it says what I've always thought, that Luke likes boys more than he likes girls

What gives you the right to put down such lies about me? Just keep well away from me!

and he thinks this will be really awful for Mum and Dad, and he says that he really does care about them, even though he's always giving them dirty looks – especially Mum – because they won't leave him alone as much as he'd like. Now I've found out one secret about Luke,

No, no, you stole a stupid letter of mine. Stole it!

but that's OK because he's got at least ninety-nine others. If not more. Luke saves up secrets. His whole life is one big secret. So secret, that when he gets home he never comes and sits with the rest of us to talk about how things went at school. If Mum asks about it, he always gives the same answer: 'Same as usual.' He makes a pot of tea for himself, and then runs upstairs with a steaming mug and locks himself in his room. He only comes out for a second cup of tea.

I've got to do my homework, haven't I?

Mum asked him once why he doesn't just take the teapot

upstairs with him. 'Then I'd never ever come downstairs again,' he said. So it's only thanks to that teapot that we ever get to see Luke at all.

What shall I go and do now?

So Marius, that's your game, is it? Just plonk a lie down on paper and then move on to other things? Oh, do carry on, by all means. But if you're going to start spreading stories about me, then I'll have to think again about rescuing your diary.

[SATURDAY, 16 OCTOBER 1971] Luke gave me this diary. So he must want me to write about him. OK then, here goes! I had a talk with Luke about the letter that I found and he denies everything!

I don't want to hear any more, Marius. If you don't stop going on about it, I've had enough of this.

He just stood there, lying his head off, and I can't understand why.

Stop!

What's the point of denying something he wrote down in black and white?

Hey! I'm telling you for the last time. Keep your dirty hands off me!

I'm very angry with him.

Angry? You? Haven't I got more reason to be angry? You broke into my room like a common thief and stole a letter!

I was lying on Mum's bed, watching television, and Luke brought me a glass of lemonade. He turned to go right away so I said quickly, 'Listen, I know all about it. You don't need to keep any secrets from me.'

You gave me that mocking smile of yours, and it got right up my nose.

'What are you going on about?' he asked irritably.
   I said mysteriously, 'I read all of it.'
   'Read what?' he asked.
   'The letter,' I said.
   'Which letter?'
   'The letter you wrote.'
   'I write a lot of letters,' Luke said.
   'But none as interesting as the one you wrote to Mum and Dad.'
   Then I told him which letter I was talking about.

Oh no, first of all you just lay there, teasing me by saying, 'Wouldn't you like to know?' Then at long last you said that you were talking about a rough draft that you'd found 'lying about' in my room.

He got angry right away and tried to talk about something else.

'What were you doing in my room, anyway?' he shouted. 'I don't want you going in my room, especially when I'm not there. And keep your mucky paws off my things!'

You had the cheek to say, 'You shouldn't leave things lying about like that.'

Then he started to spin some story about how he thought girls were really great.

Honestly, I'm not lying, I think girls are really fantastic.

'Great enough to go to bed with?' I asked.

'It's stupid just to see girls as playthings to have sex with!' Luke shouted.

But I told him that I wasn't talking about women's liberation. I was talking about what a boy and girl did with each other in bed, and that had nothing to do with female emancipation and all that.

'Not at the present time,' he said. What a really stupid remark that was!

Oh come on, I was only just fourteen!

He wouldn't talk about it any more. Just so long as he doesn't think I'm stupid, because he needn't expect me to believe now that he'd rather do it with girls. I saw that letter with my own eyes and I just can't bear the thought that Luke is lying to me.

I'm really amazed that you wrote all this down in your diary. I would never have started my rescue operation if I'd known. It may be important that your thoughts should be preserved but not if they're a load of nonsense. I'm not sure if I really want to read and write any more. . .

That's always been his trouble. He only has two solutions for everything, keep quiet or lie.

Only if I can't or won't tell the truth for some reason.

There was a time when Luke and I had no secrets from each other.

Of course we did.

We used to tell each other everything then.

Oh no we didn't.

But not any more. Not for a long time now. Luke shuts himself away in his room all day and if I dare to stick my head round the door he looks daggers at me. I don't think there's anything special about being brothers any more. I think he's a prick because he never has any time for me.

Sorry, dickhead.

I want to tell him something important but I never get the chance. He just sits in his room and draws all day long. I really wish I knew what I wanted to do and

But I really don't know for sure! Everyone automatically thinks that I'll go to art school without ever asking what I think about it. The truth is that drawing is the only thing I can do, and so I suppose I'll just *have* to become an artist.

could work at my future career every evening, like Luke does, but I just don't know what I want to be. I only know the careers that I don't want and I'm not going to write down the whole list from Architect to Zookeeper. It'll be best if I just write down the careers that might possibly appeal to me, which are:

   — Archaeologist, because you can scratch about in the earth and dig up souvenirs of history.

– Captain in the Navy, even though I don't like the military side of it. But being the captain of a ferry or barge seems so boring.

– Explorer, although I don't think there are any countries left to be explored. But discovering a star in space would be really good too.

Something to do with geography, anyway, because that's my favourite subject. The word 'erosion' is more beautiful than the most beautiful poem. And 'marshes'. That sounds just like land that's sneezing.

You're right.

[SATURDAY, 12 NOVEMBER 1971] This evening Luke and I were at home on our own.

Not about us again, surely?

We watched television together and Luke made salmon mayonnaise for me and spread it on bread, because I can't do that sort of thing myself at the moment because of my trembling.

I used to get really nervous when you opened tins and your trembling fingers came close to the razor-sharp edges. That's why I preferred to do it myself. And anyway, you always used to mash the whole tin in the mayonnaise without taking out the bones first, and the nasty bits of skin. I didn't like it so much then.

I felt that the right moment had come to raise the subject again and I decided not to beat about the bush. I said, 'I think I'm in love with a boy.' And do you know what that dumb Luke said?

What?

'Good. Isn't that nice.'

I don't think I said that.

'I'm being serious,' I said.
    'You're just imagining it.'
    'What do you mean, imagining it?'
    'You're only just thirteen,' Luke said. 'You can't be sure about that sort of thing yet.'

Did I really say that?

'And of course you'd know all about it because you're all of fourteen, I suppose?' I said, trying to get him mad on purpose.

You'd better co-operate if you want me to hang on to this diary.

'Don't be so stupid,' he shouted. 'I'm in love with Helke.'

'What about that letter, then?'

'Shut up about that letter,' Luke said. 'I thought I was in love with a boy in my class but then I fell in love with Helke. I was all mixed up. I was just practising with that letter. It was never a proper letter.'

Did I say that? Yes, I expect I did.

This was a completely different answer from the one he gave me first of all so I had proof that he'd been lying. But I didn't get any further with him.

'You're probably just trying to find yourself,' he said. 'It's perfectly normal.'

I could have shot him there and then. My brother, who was just a year older than me, was treating me as if I was a toddler. If he hadn't had such a friendly look on his face, I'd have kicked him where it hurts.

I've thought about it a lot during the past week, because if Luke and I are both that way, then it must be because of our upbringing,

Rubbish. You shouldn't believe that sort of thing.

and so it isn't our fault.

That sort of thing isn't anyone's fault.

I thought that we'd found a reason to be brothers again, just like we used to be, but Luke didn't see it that way. To be honest, I'd already imagined the day when Luke and I would skip along to Mum and Dad together and give them the good news: 'We're both gay. Isn't that nice?'

Crazy!

But Luke said, 'You've always got a girlfriend.'

I said, 'I really like girls but I'm in love with a boy.'

'That can happen sometimes,' said Luke. 'But can't you be in love with a girl too?'

'I was once.'

'There you are then!' Luke said. 'You've just happened to fall in love with a boy between girls.'

But it didn't add up to me. My longing to be with Alex

Alex? Surely you don't mean *our* Alex, who used to live down the street? Atlas-Alex?

is at least a hundred million times greater than my longing for Marjan. She's really just for show, so that everyone can see I really can have a girlfriend if I want one.

Still, I knew it was best to say nothing because Luke could well be right. After all, I'd only realised that I might be that way inclined because I'd fallen in love with Alex. But I really couldn't let Luke decide for me that it would blow over, just

*like that. Or is he really saying that what I'm feeling isn't
genuine? And that's an insult, because it really is genuine. And
I won't allow it to be snatched away as easily as that!*

Right you are, then.

*[SATURDAY, 15 JANUARY 1972] I don't understand what's
going on. Last year Luke and I had a talk*

Can't you write about something else for a change? Why don't
you write about Atlas-Alex if you were so head-over-heels in
love with him? Why are you always going on about me?

*and ever since then he's behaved as though I don't exist any
more. He stays in his room the whole time. Or else he's up on
the roof somewhere or in a tree. At least then he knows he's
shaken me off because I'm scared of heights.*

I climb because I like it. It's got nothing to do with your
fear of heights.

*I did ask him once why he spent so much time climbing things.
His answer didn't get me anywhere: 'Because I can do it.'*

That's right, because I can do it. That's all. (If I don't get
into art school, I can always become a steeplejack.)

Now, whenever he comes downstairs to watch television and he sees that I'm in the room, he goes straight back upstairs again. Have I got the plague or something?

Oh dear, I didn't realise you'd noticed. Sorry, Maus.

I thought that if I told Luke that I might be one of those, he'd find it easier to admit that he was one too. But no way. It's had just the opposite effect. It's as if I've chased him away!

What can I say to that now?

I do really want to talk to him about what's happening to me and about the way I feel, but I can't. But it isn't fair to blame Luke for this because I'm finding it very difficult at the moment to find the words for what I want to say. No, that's not quite right. I can find the words all right, and I can write them down too, but I just can't say them out loud. A moment before I want to say the word, I suddenly think that it isn't right or that I'm going to make a mistake. And even when I've written a word down and I look at it, I suddenly don't know how to pronounce it. Take a word like 'domestic', for instance. I know perfectly well that it's pronounced 'do-mes-tic' but then I suddenly begin to have doubts. Isn't it really 'dome-stick'? And because I'm scared of making a fool of myself, I decide to keep my mouth shut instead. I don't know if it's because of my trembling or because I'm becoming an adult.

I've heard that adults lose their powers of imagination, so maybe it's that. Who knows?

You grew more and more quiet. You used to start a sentence and then stop halfway, fix a Mona Lisa smile on your face, and fall mysteriously silent. Was it because you had lost the word you wanted to say? I used to think that you did it just to tease. It was as if you knew exactly what you were doing, that smile making it clear that you just didn't want to say anything to us.

For nearly a year now, Mum has been dragging me from one doctor to another. And it's always the same old story. First of all, the bloke prods my body all over with his fingers and says that he can't find anything the matter with me. Then he looks at Mum, who shoots him a really dirty look because doctors who can't find anything wrong are just quacks as far as she's concerned. And then suddenly he knows exactly what's wrong.

Oh, let me guess, Maus! May I? May I? 'Madam, if I had a mother like you, I'd go out of my mind too.' Something like that, Maus? Was it something like that?

The home situation is not ideal and I'm not getting enough attention. So I'm psychologically off-balance and it's this that is causing my trembling. That's what they all say.

[SUNDAY, 13 FEBRUARY 1972] There was a time

You've missed out my birthday, Maus.

*when I wanted to be a sea captain (or better still, a pirate –
I'm going to the carnival dressed as a pirate),*

Don't remind me about that. Alex was with you and he
really hurt my feelings by telling me to clear off. Now I
come to think of it, I never really liked Alex.

*but now I couldn't even captain a rowing boat, let alone
anything else. It's got to the point where all my wobbling is
making me seasick.*

By now your entire left arm was shaking and sometimes,
only sometimes, your head would start to tremble gently too.

When I look back, I'm amazed how slowly you
deteriorated in the beginning. We had all the time in the
world to get used to it.

*It's as if swirling clouds are racing through my body at top
speed. And I have the feeling that I'm always on the point of
drowning. And I think that the reason why my muscles ache
so much is because I hunch my shoulders, even though I've
seen in the mirror that I hardly ever do this. And I'm sick and
tired of everyone trying to draw me out, whether I like it or*

not: 'And how are things with you today?' 'Have you got any problems?' 'Is everything all right at school?' 'What exactly is the matter with you?' And then I really do hunch my shoulders, because I don't know, I don't know, I don't know! I wish they'd all just listen to me for once! And Mum and Luke are always rowing about it. Mum shouts at him that I'm ill and, because he thinks it's awful for me if she says this out loud, Luke shouts back that I've just got problems, that's all.

I thought Mum meant you were crazy and I felt this must be so awful for you. She dragged you from one doctor to another, and then called them names when they couldn't find anything wrong with you.

And I don't shout anything at all.

And all the doctors sang in chorus: 'You're daft, you're potty, you're barmy, you ought to join the army, you got knocked out with a Brussels sprout, you're daft, you're potty, you're barmy.'

I keep well out of it because I don't know, either. And Dad just shrugs it all off. Whenever he gets the chance he escapes to the garage to sort through clothes that have been collected for Africa. Luke asked him, 'Wouldn't it be easier all round if they just went about in the nude, like they used to, especially as it's so hot out there anyway? Or wouldn't God approve of that any more?' He got a slap round the ears but that didn't worry him. He said to me: 'We're both unsteady on our pins now!'

I can't remember ever saying anything like that but I do know that your 'trouble' was driving Dad mad. We were all getting a bit jumpy because of your constant trembling. But at the same time we were getting used to it.

The carnival is really good, except for Luke. He gets terribly embarrassed about going out all dressed up.

Mum said that I had to go because she thought you were too young to be out all by yourself. There really wasn't any need, because Alex was with you and he could easily look after you for a bit.

But Mum said that he had to go because she wanted to get him out of the house just for once. Alex (as a clown) and I sang and danced our way down the street, followed by Luke in a big raincoat of Dad's and a hat and a pair of large sunglasses. I thought he was meant to be a child molester.

No, a spy, you idiot!

He shuffled down the street behind us, complaining loudly the whole time, and then Alex said to him, 'Why don't you just go and crawl under a stone somewhere? You're spoiling everything for us, going around with a face like that, so I'd rather you just pissed off!'

Luke was really offended by this. He hesitated for a moment and then shouted, 'Piss off yourself, you and your stupid carnival! I go around in disguise every day as it is!'

Did I really say that? I don't know any more.

Then he turned round and walked away in a huff. I thought it was awful of Alex to send Luke off but we had a really good time after that.

Oh, great.

[TUESDAY, 15 FEBRUARY 1972] This carnival is the best there's ever been in my entire life! I've just got to get this down, even though I'm finding it more and more difficult to write. My left side is shaking so much now that I can't keep my right side properly still any more.

It's still easy to read, Maus. A bit shaky here and there, that's all.

It has happened at last! When Alex and I came back from the carnival yesterday, he wanted to show me a new atlas he'd bought. We lay down on the floor to look at it. I asked why Antarctica is at the bottom of the world even though no one knows where the top of the universe is. Maybe the South Pole is really the North Pole and we've been living the wrong way up for centuries.

This made Alex laugh and then the thing happened that I've been dreaming about for so long. He put his arm around me and gave me a kiss on the cheek. And I gave him a kiss on the cheek too and he gave me another kiss back that was half on my mouth. I tried to signal with my eyes what I wanted so much, and my message must have got through. We started to make love and didn't stop until much, much, much later.

I thought at first that we wouldn't be able to manage it because of the shaking that hardly ever leaves me now. But we were caught in a sort of vice that bound us tightly together with a force that would hurt ordinary people, and my tremor flashed like lightning right through Alex and the floor and into the earth. Yes, thunder and lightning stormed between us, and we were overwhelmed by a wild feeling that wasn't there before. We wanted to get as near to each other as we could but even that didn't seem close enough. You can't get any closer than pressing against each other, but we held each other yet more tightly so as to get closer still. To start with we had to get out of our costumes, of course, because clothes created a distance between us. He pulled the pirate clothes from me and I peeled away his clown costume. Our skins acted like magnets, drawing one to the other so closely that it seemed as if all the air between us had been sucked away. Alex clasped me in his arms and I didn't know what to do with my hands so I put them everywhere, as if I

*wanted to feel every single naked part of him. Perhaps I thought
that I could really learn to know him now.*

*You never know for sure that another boy has a cock until
you see it. Or feel it! I felt his cock pressing against my stomach
and my own cock pressing just as firmly against his, but the
strange thing was that I couldn't really tell which of the two was
mine and which was Alex's. I could feel the two of them and
they both belonged to us. We moved our hips back and forth,
and our stalks caught fast, one behind the other, then sprang
free, then hooked together again – it was as if our bodies had
been made for each other. Everything matched so exactly that
we must have been meant to be together. I can't explain it any
other way. In duels in films, men brandish their swords as they
try to stab each other; Alex and I had a kind of swordfight too,
only between us there was peace.*

*I now know for certain that falling in love with a boy isn't
just a passing phase with me. It's forever!*

I don't know how you had the nerve to write all that down! I
would never have dared. And I wouldn't have known the
words to use so that I could write about something like that.

I really want to find Luke and tell him all about it,

It's not that I'm embarrassed by those stalks of yours, but
even so, I did get the feeling that I was peering through a
keyhole. I'm not sure that I really want to know all that,

because it makes me feel like a Peeping Tom. But the really embarrassing thing is that I never noticed what was going on between you and Alex. It was as if I was deliberately looking the other way.

but talking is getting so difficult now, and the door of Luke's room is shut, which means that he doesn't want a visit from me.

I'm listening now, Maus, and I'm asking myself whether you would really want this diary to be saved. The first burglar who came along could steal it and read everything you've just told me.

Give me a sign, if you can. Let me know what you want me to do. Do you want your diary to be saved, or do you want it sent up to you in smoke? You must choose, Maus.

Oh well, it doesn't really matter.

Or do you want me to choose? I'm not sure that I can.

Luke wouldn't believe me anyway.

But I do. I do believe you, Maus!

[SUNDAY, 5 MARCH 1972] Today I woke up,

Many happy returns of your fourteenth birthday!

It still seems a bit strange – tonight I've congratulated you on your thirteenth and fourteenth birthdays. And also the first birthday when you weren't here yourself.

shaking even more.

I think we already knew by then that your shaking was officially called a tremor. Or did that come later?

I just can't keep still, however hard I try. I'm starting to look more and more like a doddery old gentleman. And I've noticed that I can't keep ideas in my head so easily any more.

And things were getting steadily worse at school. Your eights and nines had become fives and sixes. The Principal came to complain that some of the teachers were getting annoyed by your behaviour in class. Your shaking was disrupting the lessons and, as if this wasn't bad enough, you sat there with a stupid grin on your face the whole time too.

I do get ideas but the shaking seems to loosen them and I realise I've already forgotten something I thought of thirty seconds ago. It used to happen before, from time to time. I'd set out for the kitchen, for example, and start to think about something else on the way and then forget why I'd come into the kitchen. That sort of thing happens several times a day now. That's why I've decided to write things down, because it makes them easier to remember.

Now I don't know what I wanted to write about. . .

I dropped a mug this morning because I couldn't hold on to it any more. Just put it down, I said to myself. But it was already too late. It wobbled out of my hand because I can't keep my fingers tight any more. Oh well, I suppose things just aren't too good with me at the moment.

I still can't remember what I wanted to write about. Oh yes, I know now, it's my birthday today. How stupid of me. But I hadn't really forgotten that it's my birthday today, I'd just forgotten that I wanted to write it down! I'm fourteen now. And what did I get? One pathetic little hair under my nose. If I had three of them, I'd let them grow and then make them into a plait.

Yes, you were getting more and more confused but you still carried on smiling like the Mona Maus by Leonardo da Vinci. I thought maybe you really were disturbed, because you kept on smiling calmly at the most terrible news on television, as if nothing troubled you any more.

I got a portable radio from Mum and Dad. Alex – he's so sweet – gave me an old worn-out pre-war atlas, in which East and West Germany were still one country and had territory in Poland. I haven't looked at it properly yet – I didn't like to say that it doesn't interest me as much any more. Luke gave me a Joni Mitchell LP because I think 'Both Sides Now' is so beautiful.

That LP is mine now.

[MONDAY, 3 APRIL 1972] I wanted to talk to Luke so much about all the things that have been happening to me (24 times so far!),

Yes Maus, I get the message, ok?

but I can't shift the blame on to him as easily as that because sometimes when he wants to talk to me – about something on television, say – I just can't get the words out of my mouth. Like yesterday evening, for instance. It was like being proper brothers again, though a bit late in the day.

I watch a lot of television at the moment because there's not much else I can do, and Luke comes out of his room to sit with me more and more now. I really like that, because we can be together without having to talk to each other.

I really wanted to be alone but you didn't want that. And because you were a whole lot quieter than me then, we were both satisfied. We were on our own together.

Yesterday we were watching a show in which a gypsy orchestra appeared. Luke and I looked at each other and I could tell from his face that he was thinking the same as me. He got up and came and sat down on the sofa beside me. We felt really close, just as we always used to. He even put his arm around my shoulders.

I'd seen from your expression that we were thinking the same thing too. It felt very chummy all of a sudden.

And we didn't need to say anything.

We both knew what we'd been thinking about.

We were seven and eight years old then, I think.

Something like that, yes. Eight and nine to be precise.

And there was a gypsy camp

I was right! I knew we were thinking the same thing.

on the corner near our house.

On the waste ground. There used to be a beautiful house there at one time. I can still vaguely remember it.

We were really rather scared of the gypsies

Thanks to the other children at school.

and I don't think Mum liked that.

Mum said that it was ridiculous to be scared of gypsies.

She said that she was a gypsy herself under her bleached hair, and we believed her.

You bet we did! It was so exciting to have a mother who was a gypsy.

But we had to keep it a secret because Dad must never find out that he'd married a gypsy.

And so we went and spied on the gypsies from the bushes because we wanted to know what life would have been like if Mum had married a man of her own people instead of a farmer's son from the country.

We had no reason to think that our Mum was lying because we'd often noticed that her hair was dark when the colour grew out, and we'd seen how she then hurriedly hid her gypsy tresses under blonde dye. But oh, what a beautiful secret it was!

Yes, because no one knew either that we were the only two

fair-haired gypsy children in the world. We didn't need to dye our hair to keep the secret.

We felt pretty special because we weren't just ordinary boys who happened to end up with a mother and father who had found us in the bushes. We were real gypsy children.

That doesn't sound quite right to me, Maus. You're mixing up two different stories. First of all, Mum told us that we were the descendants of gypsies. Then, later on, I asked her if she was my real mother, and she said, 'Marius is my real child and I found you in the bushes, but I love you both.' And then, when you asked Mum if she was your real mother, she said, 'Luke was found in the bushes but I stole you from a pram.' From the way she said it, we didn't really believe her but even so, we were never completely certain.

Luke and I used to go and lie in the bushes and watch the camp, because we'd heard at school that gypsies kidnapped children and came to steal the silver tableware. So we had a very exciting 'real' family.

We stared at the gypsy children. They had black hair, and strings of snot hanging from their noses. Oh, if only we'd been allowed strings of snot too! But that was impossible, of course, because then Dad would have noticed right away that we were really gypsy children and Mum would have been betrayed. If ever we were troubled by runny noses, we had to take out our handkerchiefs at once.

I asked Luke why gypsies only came to steal children and silver cutlery. He didn't know anything about the children but he did know that, whenever they have visitors, gypsies like to lay silver knives, forks and spoons on the grass round the camp-fire, just like people who live in ordinary houses.

Except we use tables, of course.

Like us.

I just made all that up, because we only bring out the silver cutlery on Sundays and special occasions.

Luke also said that gypsies melt down any cutlery that's left over and make earrings from it.

Well, I thought, what else would they do with all those knives and forks? No one has *that* many visitors.

One day, one of the older gypsy boys came right up to the very spot where we were lying in the bushes.

He came right up to us. We lay there, shaking with fear and

clutching each other by the hand, because we'd never before been so close to a thief who stole silver and children.

We were almost beside ourselves with terror, longing to run away, but we stayed where we were, not daring to move. We had just seen a nature programme on television in which very young deer kept still so as not to be discovered. But those animals had been in a black-and-white television landscape, of course, while we were in colour.

Wearing bright red sweaters in the green bushes.

He had thick eyebrows like two half-moons, a moustache,

He was sixteen or seventeen, I think.

and flashing eyes.

Dark flashing eyes. He looked so very different from us, two small white-haired streaks of nothing.

He crept into the bushes and we hardly dared breathe, because he was standing only a few metres away. Suddenly he caught sight of us, and gave a start. He began to talk to us excitedly in a language that we didn't understand and we got really scared then. We thought he was threatening us and so we fled, screaming at the tops of our voices. As I ran, it suddenly struck me that I could only hear my own footsteps. I looked round but I couldn't see Luke anywhere and so I stopped a little further on to see what had happened to him. Luke was sitting up in a tree. The gypsy boy was standing at the bottom, still talking. He beckoned to Luke. Perhaps Luke was scared that he might have to stay up in the tree all night because he climbed down again.

I climbed down because I'd noticed that the gobbledegook coming from his mouth didn't sound at all threatening. And he wasn't clenching his fists but beckoning to me in a friendly way. And there was something in his eyes that drew me down to the ground again. I knew perfectly well that Mum and Dad had told me never to go anywhere with strange men. But he wasn't a man; he was a gypsy boy. One of us, after all.

The gypsy boy took Luke by the hand and led him away.

He took my hand, pushed it against his chest three, four times and said, 'Tibor, Tibor, Tibor.' I understood that this was his name but I didn't dare tell him mine.

We sat down on the grass and he carried on talking.

I thought that the gypsy boy was going to steal Luke and I ran home as fast as I could.

I listened open-mouthed, even though I understood nothing that he said. For some reason or other, this didn't seem to matter. I stared at his big dark eyes with their long lashes, at the thin moustache under his nose, and at his eyebrows. They looked as if they had been put on with soot; I had never seen such black hair so close at hand before. I also saw that there was no string of snot, and no silver ring in his ear. He picked some flowering clover and showed me how to weave a garland with it.

In a complete panic, I pulled the cutlery drawers from the sideboard and emptied them into a bag. Then I ran back and lay in wait, all set to be brave when the gypsies came to lock Luke away. I would then leap forward and offer the silver in exchange for my brother.

How touching!

I'd decided that we could manage perfectly well with the ordinary cutlery from the kitchen but we couldn't do without Luke. Luckily, it wasn't necessary. Luke and the boy were sitting on the grass, weaving flowers. Luke saw me and beckoned to me to come closer, but I didn't dare. Then he came running up to me and asked what was in the bag.

'Nothing,' you said.

I shrugged my shoulders.

For as long as I can remember, it's been my job to put the silver tidily back in the drawers after washing-up, and so I was angry at first when I looked inside the bag and saw the cutlery in such a muddle.

'What have you done that for?' I asked haughtily. Twelve knives, twelve forks and twelve spoons, twelve dessert knives, twelve dessert forks and twelve dessert spoons, twelve fish knives, three serving spoons, one soup ladle, one set of salad servers, six lobster forks, two sauce ladles, two meat forks and a cake slice were all jumbled up in a heap. And as you didn't know one end of the cutlery drawers from another, *I* was the one who'd have to put everything back again in its proper place.

Luke got really nasty and so I said that I'd gone to fetch the silver so that I could do a swap. My brother for the cutlery.

I thought that was really sweet.

But fortunately he didn't go back to the gypsy boy

Well, that's not quite. . .

but stayed with me instead. He did give him a wave, though. Luke took my hand and we went home together. And then he showed me where in the drawers the forks had to go, and then the knives, and the serving spoons, and so on.

And Mum stood and watched. She couldn't understand what on earth we were doing with the silver. But it was none of her business anyway.

And that's what we were both thinking about as we listened to the gypsy orchestra on television.

I think that was the very last time we played together.

When we played with the silver cutlery, you mean? Perhaps you're right.

Luke went to live in trees and on rooftops, behind closed doors. Anywhere that I couldn't go. We were still brothers but we weren't togetherish brothers any more.

Togetherish. That's a good word you've invented, Maus.

And we weren't friends any more, either.

But we never were friends, Maus. Not really. You choose your friends or else they choose you. We were brothers; we hadn't chosen each other and so we didn't make any effort with each other. We could call each other all the names under the sun and wipe the floor with each other afterwards without ever having to worry that we would stop being brothers because of it. Friends can always keep out of each other's way but brothers can never be free of each other. After every quarrel they still have to live under the same roof.

I was so used to having you around that I never once asked myself what being brothers really meant. When we were both still alive, if anyone had asked me what exactly brothers were, I would probably have said that brothers have the same parents, that they had to be on the alert all day long to make sure that the other one didn't get a larger slice of cake, and that they always got in each other's way.

If we'd been friends instead of brothers, then I might have grieved as much, but sooner or later I'd have gone in search of another friend. And maybe I'd have been lucky enough to find one. The difference is that I can't go out and look for another brother, even if there was one to be found.

It was a cosy evening, even though we didn't say anything at all.

Not with our voices, no.

There was a time when I couldn't keep my mouth still,

That's one of the reasons why I came out of my room again: we were gradually becoming two silent brothers. I thought that was really good.

and now I can't keep my body still. And I've really had enough of it.

I know, Maus.

[SATURDAY, 19 MAY 1972] There are gaps in my thoughts and my memory and it confuses me. If I don't write down all the things I do from time to time, then I can't find my way through my own head any more. Because there are times when I suddenly forget what day it is or what you use a cheese grater for. I'm scared that I'll say something really crazy because sometimes when I say something, words come out of my mouth that I don't really mean.

Mum kept dragging you from doctor to doctor because the tremor had taken hold of your entire body and because you were becoming so confused. It's all in the mind, they insisted.

By the end of May, you couldn't really go to school any more; your tremor was making it difficult for the other students and the teachers to concentrate, your writing was rapidly becoming illegible (that doesn't surprise me; I've got used to your scrawl, thanks to all this reading) and they couldn't teach you any more. And I really do mean they couldn't teach you any more. You couldn't give an answer to the simplest questions. You'd look as if you were searching inside your head, then you'd sit down in silence with that irritating Mona Maus smile on your mug.

At mealtimes you had to use a plastic plate and plastic cutlery, not because we minded you breaking plates and glasses but because you'd already injured your mouth by smashing a glass on your teeth, and because you'd pricked your cheek with your fork, leaving four drops of blood in a neat row. In the end Mum had to feed you.

But the mocking smile remained. And that puzzling expression... And the mysterious silence. It was as if Mona Maus was teasing us.

Actually there isn't much point in writing anything at all because my handwriting is such a scrawl now, thanks to my tremor.

I used the same word quite by chance: scrawl! But I can still read it, Maus, so it's not as bad as all that.

Luckily my right-hand side doesn't shake quite as badly as the left, because I've noticed when I'm writing that the only problem is keeping my concentration. I have to think about what I'm writing and how it comes out on the paper and this collects all the rubbish in my head into one place. I don't know how it works but it's only on paper that I'm not split into pieces. Somehow or other I manage to pull myself together and make proper sentences again. It takes me ages to get a sentence finished, but every sentence without any mistakes is proof that I'm not crazy. I am not crazy. But everyone thinks I am. All the doctors have said that I'm psychologically off-balance on account of emotional deprivation at home. Mum is really furious that the doctors have said this, because she sees it as an accusation. 'They're out of their minds!' she yells. 'Marius is ill, that's all, terribly ill!' And then Luke flares up, because he thinks it's awful for me if Mum says that out loud. He keeps shouting that I've got psychological problems, that's all.

I can't stand it any more. I suppose I should be glad that Dad keeps out of the way but that's not much help, either. Mum and Luke's bickering about my condition at least shows that they care about me. Alex does too, even though we don't go to bed with each other any more.

Oh? Why not?

My tremor has got too bad now and it only fades away when I'm asleep (so I've been told, because I'm asleep at the time!). He's really sweet to me but my shaking is driving him frantic. Perhaps he's getting a bit tired of me too. I write him letters sometimes, but I haven't posted a single one of them. I always tear them up. Because it's more important for me to put into words what I feel than it is to bore Alex with them. He said that he isn't in love with me any more but he still likes me. I'm just as crazy about him as I was in the beginning, even though we don't make love any more. At least this means that someone who's gay is still homosexual even if he isn't having sex. Or is the word homophile?

I think that homophile is the old word and homosexual the new one and they both mean the same thing.

[MONDAY, 4 JUNE 1972] I'm sick of everything everyone!

Everything *and* everyone, you mean.

All the things they say to me are bursting with quesnot marks.

Quesnot marks? Oh, question marks.

Questions, questions, questions, and I don't know the answers. Have you got any problems? Are you feeling happy? Have you been to the doctor? Yes, for the hindredth time. I've been to the doctor, ten doctors at least, and they all say the same thing. And I don't want to talk about it any more. And I can't any more, anyway. Sometimes I'd like to shoot everyone

Maus, please.

so that I can have some peace and get to sleep. But thanks to this tremblingbling of mine I'd only manage to shoot an ear off here or a fingernail there and it wouldn't be tecause because I want to slowly torture everyone. I'd want to get it over in one go. And now I can hardly do anything for myself any more and I've been excluded from school.

You weren't excluded from school, though it may have felt as if you were. You were officially allowed to stay at home: 'permissible absence', I think it's called. They'd pay a fortune for a certificate like that on the student black market!

I I just sit staring into space the whole time or watching television, or I sleep. Much against the wishes of Alex and Luke. They pluck me out of the chair to go out walkinging, so that at least I'm doing something. Even though I don't want to go anywhere. Even breathing is a tiring business now.

[SUNDAY, 23 JUNE 1972] I really don't want to write any more because I make such strange mistakes. As if I'm a stupid idiot. And I'm so tired all the time. Shaking all day long wears me out so. I want to sleep so badly but it's hard when your body is jerking the whole time. You're never at rest. Luckily, I slept well last night and so I don't feel so terribly tired today. Who knows, perhaps I've turned the corner at last and things will get better from now on. Wouldn't that be great? And I haven't made a single mistake in what I've written so far. Yes, things can only get better from now on, I'm quite sure of that. And the sun's shining today. That's a good sign too. Luke pulled me out of the chair, upsadaisy, to go out of doors with him. We walked – or rather, he walked and dragged me behind him – to the field on the corner. I saw the buttercups, the daisies, the dandelions and the stinging nettles all doing their best to

exist. And I thought to myself, I wish that I wanted to exist. I was feeling so tired again.

'Let's have a little rest,' Luke said, and we sat down where we were, halfhalfway across the field. Luke picked white clover and wove it into a garland for me. It was so good to see how calmly and peacefully Luke made the garland. His hands were so beautifully still. Even in the days when my hands were still, I could never do all that fidfiddling with my fingers. I could never have done that, even if he showed me a hundred times.

Tibor taught me.

I don't think I'll ever learn how to do it. Luke must have shown me a hundred times how to mend a bicycle puncture and I never even thanked him for it. I was on the point of telling him

Don't worry about it.

that I thought it was awful that he had to look out for me as well as seeing to his own chores. I know that he hates it but he doesn't say anything.

You don't hear me complaining.

But I didn't.

I still have so much to tell you.

Everything I say comes out wring wrong. So I kept quiet and watched as Luke finished the garland of clover and put it on my head. And of course my tremor shook it off in no time at all but that was no problem. Luke simply made it a bit longer so that he could hang it round my neck.

I lied, Maus.

It was so beautifully quiet. The tops of the poppers poplars rustled so cheerfully and Luke didn't climb any of the trees. He stayed by my side and we smiled at each other. Luckuckily we didn't need any words.

Don't go!

Perhaps when the timeco comes the comestime, the time, hang on, take it slowly now. Perhaps when the time comes to pick the cherries, I'll be well enough to help him.

Here I am again. I've had to leaf through the diary to find an empty page, because the first page that I filled up followed the last words that you wrote.

I wanted to carry on writing straight away but suddenly it was so hot in my room that I had to open a window. I'd been puffing away all night and the smoke from a good twenty or thirty roll-ups shot outside. I could still hear some late carnival revellers in the distance.

I went and sat out on the roof for a bit, and looked up at the dark blue night filled with stars. Suddenly, they seemed to be shining even more brightly. No, it wasn't a miracle, it was just that I was having a quiet howl to myself and my eyes had filled with tears. I've read everything that you've written and there isn't any more, and so it felt as though I'd lost you all over again. Stupid, isn't it? Because I've never felt as close to you as I do now. Closer even than the evening when we listened to the gypsy orchestra together.

It's as if you've come to visit me in my room, even

though I can't see you anywhere. But it's also as if I've paid you a visit on your birthday, although I don't know where. Do you understand what I mean?

But I'm glad that you've stayed a little while, Maus, because there's so much that I must tell you. Starting with this: I lied to you. It wasn't because I couldn't tell the truth, but because I didn't want to. Because if I tell you the truth, I'm left with a problem. I wanted to save your diary so that your thoughts will be preserved, but in your diary there is a secret that you stole from me, and it's important that my secrets remain secret. I don't think this will be possible if the diary is here for just anyone to read.

Still, I don't want to lie to you any more. I want you to know the truth, even if this means that I must let your diary be burned. And then this rescue mission will have failed.

Listen, Maus. When I was little, I soon realised that I was different from other children. I thought that I was a very special little boy and that the other boys were jealous of me because they themselves were so ordinary. That was why they teased me and gave me the cold shoulder, although there was always someone who wanted to be my friend. I didn't find it so bad at first, because I knew of course that I didn't belong: I felt that I had been specially chosen to be different.

I realised later that they didn't think me different in the sense of being special but in the sense of being apart. To start with, I didn't behave like the other boys. If they played football, I would sit and draw. When they played tag, I was busy modelling clay. That's why I didn't belong with them; they thought I was crazy. They sang about it too: 'You're daft, you're potty, you're barmy, you ought to join the army, you got knocked out with a Brussels sprout, you're daft, you're potty, you're barmy.'

Some people called me a 'girl' because I always used to pinch the others when we had fights instead of punching them. Pinching was seen to be vicious, and only girls fought viciously. They had their own school across the street; that's where I belonged.

I was eight when I realised that being special had something to do with feelings. My feelings seemed different from those of ordinary boys. They weren't in love with the teacher of Class Three and I was, so it was best that I kept that a secret. Especially as Mr Brink seemed to have taken a dislike to me, worse luck. He called me out in front of the class one day and pointed to a piece of dictation I'd done.

'What sort of letter do you call that?' he boomed.

'A "d", sir.'

'That isn't a "d"!' he shouted angrily. 'A "d" has a stick, not a curl. Go and write it out a hundred times.'

It took very little effort for me to hate him after that, because I'd copied the beautiful 'd' with a curl on top from – Mr Brink himself! He was paying me back for stealing his 'd.'

At that time the teasing from some of the boys turned into bullying. They hid my coat (so that I had to spend half an hour searching for it), they threw my bicycle keys in a ditch, they pricked me in the back with compasses, and they chased after me with sticks. You know the sort of thing. Well, no, of course you don't, because you were really popular at school. They all wanted to be friends with you.

Luckily, (for me if not for him) there was always a boy in the class who was seen to be even more stupid than I was and who was less able to cope with the teasing, so I wasn't always the victim. The boys would never admit it but each time I won the hundred-metre race or was the first to climb the rope in gym, I earned a bit more respect. Of course they always said that I'd cheated but the truth was really quite simple: I had learned to run faster and climb higher than those who were chasing me. And they had to admit that I could draw really well.

Just as they thought it odd that I had no time for sport and cars, so did I find it strange that all those boys, none of whom was yet ten years old, wanted to stare at naked girls. What was so nice about that? Don't worry, I wasn't *that* stupid; I knew perfectly well that you had to go to bed with a girl if you wanted a baby. But that was something that happened later on. *Much* later on. The very idea of having sex, and with a girl at that, didn't appeal to me at all. It just seemed horribly dirty to me. The other boys behaved as though they couldn't wait to start having sex with girls and I naturally realised that just as it's normal to have children so is it normal for boys and girls to make love with each other. The fact that I didn't want to and already knew perfectly well that I'd *never* want to was therefore *not* normal, and people who weren't normal were sent to the madhouse. It would therefore be best if I kept secret the fact that I'd also fallen in love with the teacher of Class Four. I nursed this silent love because Mr Vanderwey had an eye for my drawings. And when he selected clay models to bake in the oven in handwork, there was one of mine among them more often than not. This didn't always go down well with the other boys, of course, who had to watch as their rejected ashtrays were returned to the clay bucket time after time. I had to pay dearly for this with punches and abuse, and they called me a teacher's pet. I actually thought they were right, and I wondered if the other boys had cottoned on to the fact that I was in love with Mr Vanderwey. Was I being bullied more often because of this? If so, I would have to bury my secret even deeper and act as if I really was normal. But it didn't work. I couldn't do it. I was so very bad at acting like a normal boy and so very good at being myself, that I felt a total failure. Of course that was the last thing I wanted to be so I kept telling myself proudly that I was a very special boy. And everyone had to know about it. And so they bullied me at school.

Then I shut myself up in my own room at home, where I could be the master. No one came to pester me in my room (except you, of course) and I could sit there feeling special all by myself. I drew pictures of the world as I wanted it to be. And in that world there was no place for you, who only needed to let off a fart to be invited to the next birthday party. I think I was really jealous of your popularity.

And then came the day when I climbed the tree. Tibor was standing there, beckoning me to come down. I thought he was the most beautiful person I'd ever seen. He would do me no harm, I felt sure of that. And so I climbed down the tree. I felt so proud that someone so beautiful wanted to sit with me on the grass and that he actually wove me a garland of clover! No one had ever done that for me before. He didn't chase me away because I was different, oh no, he wanted me to sit with him because I was special. I knew this without understanding a word he said.

I was in love with him but it was different from the love I felt for the teacher in front of me in class. You know that I don't like to be touched, but when Tibor stroked my head and kissed me on the cheek, I tingled all over.

You don't know this, but I saw Tibor a couple of times after that first meeting. And each time, we sat on the grass or went for a walk. He always talked nineteen to the dozen and I couldn't understand a word he said. But I didn't mind that. I didn't mind at all. When he held my hand or put his arm round me, then everything was fine.

Actually, there were two words he used a lot that I *could* understand: Lucky Luke. That's what he called me. It wasn't very original, of course, but it sounded quite different coming from him than it did from the boys at school. Tibor made it sound sweet and pleasant, with no hint of ridicule. I could take it from him. And he had such beautiful eyes and his hair was so terribly black and when he smiled his white teeth gleamed. All except one, between his front teeth and his eye-tooth. It was missing. There was a black gap there and it was a great mystery to me what had happened to that tooth. On anyone else that gap would have looked ugly but on Tibor I thought it beautiful. Because it was the only fault I could discover about him.

One day we walked to the bridge. We leaned over the railing and looked at the water that murmured underneath. He put his hand on my back as if he was scared that I might fall in. I hung even further over the bridge, my feet off the ground, in the hope that he would hold me even more tightly. And he did. He wrapped his arm round my middle. I have never felt as safe as I did then. I wanted it to last for ever. And so I leaned even further over the railing. Tibor moved behind me and bent over me, so that I couldn't possibly fall. I felt his warm body and smelled his fragrance. It was as if he had washed himself with tea.

All too soon he lifted me down to the ground. I could tell that he was trying to explain something to me because his gestures were more excitable than usual but no, I couldn't understand him. He took a piece of paper from his pocket and wrote his name on it. Then he gave me a push and pointed to the other side of the bridge. I understood that he wanted me to cross over. When I had reached the other railing, he held the piece of paper in the air and then let it fall in the water. He came running to the other side and together we peered down into the water. The note drifted past on the current. Tibor gave it a wave and I copied him. I understood perfectly what he meant but I didn't want to know about it. When he gave me a hearty embrace and kissed me at least ten times on the cheeks, I got so angry that I pulled away from him and ran home as fast as I could. I deliberately didn't look back because I knew that Tibor would wave and, even at that distance, he might have been able to see my tears.

The day after that, the field was empty. The gypsies had gone and they had taken Tibor with them. And not me.

It's too long ago now to be completely certain, but I think it was probably then that I realised for the first time what was the matter with me. I was so sorry that I had pulled away from Tibor's embrace when I really wanted nothing more than to feel his arms around me, his cheek against mine, hearing the breathing in his chest going on and on and on. Always on. I think it was then that I slowly began to realise that my heart would never beat as fast for a girl, but only for a boy. It was not a choice; it was just something that had happened to me.

I thought that I was the only boy in the world who would ever fall in love with another boy. It never entered my head that I was gay. I already knew the word, of course, because gays were dirty old scumbags who liked to play filthy sex games with little boys they lured into their clutches. I certainly didn't see myself as one of those.

When I was eleven or twelve, I saw a man being interviewed on television. He explained that he was gay and what it actually meant: he was madly in love with a man. You could only see his silhouette on the television, because they had switched the lights off. He didn't want anyone to recognise him. But I felt really embarrassed because I recognised myself. I knew exactly what he was talking about and I realised then for the first time that I might not be the only person in the world like me.

But I was shocked, even so, because I'd always thought that the only people who didn't want to be recognised on television were those who had committed a crime. So it really was as bad as that!

I hardly dared go to school the next day because I was so scared that the others might have recognised me in that shadow on television and that the lights would go out for me everywhere. And when Frank said at break that he'd once seen a real gay and even knew where he lived, I felt so miserable that I didn't know where to look. Luckily he gave an address that I didn't know. But no one pointed at me; they didn't make the connection between me and that shadow on television. Good. The lights stayed on. And I began to work out a plan to preserve my secret for good and all.

Instead of becoming an artist, it would be much better if I became a monk or a priest, because they never marry and so no one is suspicious if they don't have a wife. But I wasn't entirely happy with this idea, either. I felt pretty certain that I hadn't been put on this earth to walk around in silence, saying Hail Marys for ever and ever, amen.

What then? The only thing I could think of was to act normally. To try and fall in love with a girl, get married, have children, and then, oh yes, then life would be wonderful. And I really did do my best and kissed girls just as you did, but it was all just for show.

We had girls in the same class at secondary school, and I discovered that I preferred to hang around with them than with the boys. The girls didn't bully me and they even seemed to like me! I had no shortage of friends. We had a really good time, the girls and I, smoking roll-ups on the sly behind the bushes in the playground or sitting on the footpath while Jerome played his guitar. And Jerome smoked pot! The girls whispered that he really was the greatest, and they all wanted to kiss him. And so did I, though of course I didn't say so.

I went to the library to look for books on 'the subject', creeping around with sweat on my brow, terrified that the librarian would discover what my mission was. And at home, in bed, I tried as hard as I could to imagine what it would be like to be normal and go to bed with a girl. But even my imagination, usually so vivid, had difficulty with this. If my fantasy went any further than kissing, then the girl changed into a boy. It was hopeless! Perhaps I ought to become a monk after all. I'd been spending so much time brooding in my room or out on the roof or up in a tree, out of everyone's reach, that I was getting accustomed to being by myself. This would certainly come in very useful in a monastery.

Mum didn't approve at all. Boys of fourteen were not supposed to shut themselves in their rooms and had no need to go out on the roof. Boys of fourteen were too old to be climbing trees.

'You're so quiet and gloomy and unhappy,' Mum said, 'and I don't know how to help you.'

'I'm not unhappy,' I said. 'I'm just not happy. That's quite different.'

This was no help to her at all. Mum persuaded me to go and see a psycho (whether he was a psychiatrist or a psychologist I never did discover) and I didn't have the nerve to ask why I should.

I was ushered into the psycho's consulting room and he asked me the most impossible questions. Questions that I certainly hadn't expected and which quite upset me. Not least because the ghastly man looked as if he was bored to death.

'Do you masturbate?' His pen was poised to write down my reply.

'Pardon?' I stared at the man in astonishment. He looked even uglier than before, with that strange bush of pubic hair on his head.

'Do you play with yourself?' He thought that I didn't know the word 'masturbate' but I was too taken aback to do anything but gasp for breath. I thought: I want to tell a lie but this bloke has been trained and so he'll know when I'm lying, and if I'm not telling the truth I'll end up in the madhouse.

He was giving me such a withering look that I decided to behave as though it was a perfectly natural thing for me, and so I said, 'Yes.' (I wish now that I'd said, 'Yes, but not as often as you.')

'And what do you think about when you're doing it?'

At that moment I felt a pang of intense hatred for Mum and Dad, because I couldn't understand why they'd thought it was such a good idea for me to be asked such awful questions.

'I don't think about anything,' I lied. 'I just do it.' (I could hardly tell him that I left my window and curtains ajar when I went to bed. That I lay there pretending that a thief was crossing the street and saw my open window. The robber climbed over the gate, clambered on to the porch roof, and crept through my open window to steal the silverware. He bent over me and I felt his breath on my neck. I could smell tea, and I turned my head and looked the thief in the face. It was Tibor. I recognised him at once. And he recognised me. He fell in love then and there. He put his arms around me and forgot all about the silver. But the police were outside because the neighbours had seen Tibor sneaking through the window. The police had a megaphone and they shouted, 'Give yourself up, you dirty gypsy!' But Tibor had already surrendered to me and I to him. And together we surrendered to the police. I walked outside ahead of him, so that they would have to shoot me first if they wanted to get rid of him. I couldn't be sent to an institution because I wasn't yet sixteen, but Tibor had to go to prison because he was now an adult. I naturally went to see him and smuggled nail files inside. He spoke to me through the bars in a language I could understand. 'It's terrible in the nick,' he said, 'but luckily I have you to think about and so I'll be able to endure twenty years in my cell. But I'm scared that you won't wait for me.' I gave him a loving smile but I made a point of saying nothing because I wanted to keep him on tenterhooks in case I should run away with someone else. Beautiful, don't you think?)

'But something must get you excited, surely?' the psycho asked without looking up from his piece of paper. 'Some thought or other, perhaps?'

'Oh no,' I boasted. 'It just happens, that's all.'

'What does your favourite girl look like?'

Yet another stupid question. Did he really expect me to answer, 'She's got a downy little moustache and one tooth missing'?

'She has hair as black as ebony,' I said, 'lips as red as

blood, and skin as white as snow.' I thought: I'm describing Snow White, because Snow White has always been my favourite fairy tale. And I wasn't lying either, because Tibor had hair like that, and lips, and skin.

I can't remember any more of that conversation, just the man's stupid questions and my description of Snow White. I didn't think he had the right to interrogate me so shamefully.

When it was over I didn't dare ask Mum what it had all meant. Did she know what that terrible doctor had asked me? Not that it would have made any difference because I certainly wasn't going to talk about it. And she didn't, either. To this day I have no idea if that strange conversation yielded anything useful to Mum. Everything stayed just the way it was.

About four months after that, you turned up with the news that you'd read the rough draft of my letter. I was shocked, because I was so scared that you'd give away my secret. I could see only one way out: denial and lies.

In reality the rough draft was all part of the plan. I'd decided to forget all about the monastery and stop kidding myself any longer. I had at last resigned myself to the fact that I wasn't going to change into a normal boy. I *had* hoped that a day would come when I would have to choose, one way or the other, whether to be homo or hetero. But I really had no choice. It had already been decided for me a long time before. I simply had no say in the matter. No, the only thing that I had to decide was whether to pretend that I wasn't gay. Choosing whether to be normal or not just didn't come into it.

I could accept this because I actually liked being the way I was. I still felt that I was a really special boy and why would a special boy choose to be ordinary? But I felt sure there was no one in the world who would understand this. That's why I wanted to leave home. I'd leave a letter for Mum and Dad and then clear off, so that they couldn't respond right away. If I stayed, they might be so shocked by the news that they'd throw me out of the house, lock me in the cellar, give me a hiding, commit me to an institution. But if I was missing, I hoped that their concern would be greater than their anger. Perhaps they'd realise then that they would still love me even if I didn't provide them with any grandchildren. The only thing was that I didn't really know where to go. I had already looked for a place where I could hide but I couldn't find one. And so the letter remained just a rough draft.

Then came the evening when you brought the subject out into the open and in doing so told me that you were in love with a boy. Of course I didn't know then that you were talking about Alex.

I didn't believe a word of it. I thought that you were trying to draw me out and so I didn't take you seriously. In none of the books about sexuality that I'd read, was there any mention of more than one child in a family being homosexual. It was always just one child, and it was always emphasised that the other children in the family were dead normal. And since I knew for certain that I was the gay in our family, then it couldn't possibly be you. And anyway, your life was quite different from mine. You were never bullied, you always had plenty of friends at school, and, until you became so ill, you led a fairly happy life. How could you possibly be gay?

But it really didn't matter if I believed you or not. Now that I knew that by some quirk of fate you seemed to be gay, I had been saddled with a really major problem: how would Mum and Dad react when they found out? With two gay sons they could forget all about grandchildren and who would they blame for that? Me, of course, because I was the eldest. 'Surely you must have realised that Marius always copies everything you do? You've set a very poor example. It's all your fault that Marius is that way inclined.'

I wanted to show them that I wasn't influencing you, but would Mum and Dad believe what I'd read somewhere, that you didn't become gay, you simply *were* gay? Of course they wouldn't. And that is the reason why I shut myself in my room more often than before. I was deliberately keeping out of the way because I was scared of the accusing fingers of Mum and Dad.

But I believe you now, Maus. It wasn't an imitation. You were gay all by yourself. It's a pity that we couldn't have talked about it together before it was too late. And it was too late all too soon, thanks to your illness. I asked you once if your shaking had anything to do with preferring boys or girls. You gave me such a nasty smile that I felt there wasn't much point in talking to you about it any more.

For some reason you didn't take it all as seriously as I did. Your idea was that we should skip merrily along to Mum and Dad and say to them: 'We're both gay. Isn't that nice?' Perhaps it wasn't a problem for you and you were able to accept the fact that you had fallen in love with a boy, but why then didn't you go and tell Mum and Dad yourself? You just didn't have the nerve to do it without me.

The difference between you and me is that I knew I was different from the outset, while you only realised it when you fell in love. I've had my entire life to think about what it means to be different, to be bullied, shut out, beaten. You never had any of that.

Will Mum and Dad be as happy about it as you thought? I don't know and I don't want to take the risk. My plan is to wait until I've left home. I'll tell them once I get to art school. Then their reaction won't hurt me as much. I'll be gone. They'll have no more power over me and I'll be free to be as special as I want. I can hardly wait!

Do you think I'll get into art school? I really want to go to the Gerrit Rietveld in Amsterdam. It's one and a half hours on the train so I'll have to go into lodgings. Then I'll be my own boss at last. At last.

Now that I've told you all this and it's down in your diary in black and white, and now that Mum and Dad know that the diary exists, I've come to a decision.

I know that it's important for your thoughts to be preserved, but it's just as important that my secrets remain secret. If this diary is saved, don't you think that Mum especially will be really curious about what we've written? Particularly after all I've done to rescue the diary. How do you think she'll react if she discovers that she'll never be a grandma? That I did this to her after her other son died? After all, I'm her only hope for grandchildren now.

What is there to be gained if she finds out that you were gay too? It really doesn't make any difference now whether you fancied boys or girls because you don't love anyone at all any more. Mum and Dad might even blame themselves, because it's only natural for parents to think they've done something wrong if both their children turn out to be gay. But I don't believe it's anyone's fault.

That's why I've decided that it would be best if we don't keep your diary, so that we can keep our secrets. It's the best thing for everyone, don't you think? I'll take this diary to Mum this afternoon so that she can burn it, and I'll hang around to make sure that she doesn't read it first, on the quiet.

I feel quite glad about it, to be honest, because it means I can now play a part in a ritual that I really do think is rather beautiful. It's not that I think you'll be able to read these words in smoke, because I don't believe that heaven exists. So why do I keep on writing then? Because I've known for a long time that you're reading this over my shoulder. Don't ask me how that's possible. It's what I feel, that's all. And I'm really happy about it, because there's still so much I have to tell you.

About ten days ago we had some news, news that concerns you more than anyone, and so you ought to know about it before this diary goes up in flames. I'll start where you finished off, because I don't know how much you can still remember.

By the end of June last year you couldn't be left on your own any more. You were getting more and more confused. One evening you were determined to go and see Alex on your own. We let you go, but we rang Alex to ask him to come and meet you. He couldn't find you anywhere. We were so worried that we got in touch with the police.

At about half-past-twelve that night, Mum had a phone call from the police in Utrecht. You'd been found in a bus and the driver didn't know what to do with you. You couldn't tell him where you wanted to go. All you knew were your name and telephone number. Mum leaped into the car to go and fetch you. How you ended up in Utrecht, no one will ever know.

A couple of days later you were taken into hospital. To

the psychiatric ward. You were in a room for two to start with, but because your tremor made the bed squeak so much that your roommate nearly went out of his mind, you were moved to a single room and they screwed your bed firmly to the floor.

That first week you were still quite mobile. Mum and I took you for walks round the hospital, even though it took you a good hour to stumble round. Once, when we arrived back at the entrance to the ward, you shouted at some of your fellow patients, 'I don't belong here with all you loonies!'

A few days later Mum came home blazing with rage after visiting you. She said that she'd gone into your room and found you with your head in a half-filled washbasin. She pulled you out of the water by your hair. You said that you'd just wanted a drink and then couldn't get up again.

Mum raised an almighty stink over the fact that you had nearly drowned, in hospital of all places. She said that the nursing staff should pay more attention, but of course they couldn't station a nurse by your bed the whole time.

The holiday on the Côte d'Azur was cancelled. We didn't want to go off and enjoy ourselves in the sun while you were in hospital; we would visit you instead. But you really didn't want us there. It wasn't just because Mum was forever finding fault but because you had been prescribed a sleeping cure and this gave you the rest that you longed for. You were tired out by the shaking, and I think you were a little tired of us as well.

Mum was deeply hurt when you asked a nurse to tell her that you'd rather she didn't come to see you any more. But she resigned herself to it, more or less. I was still welcome, but more often than not you were asleep when I came. And when I looked at you and saw your body lying there motionless, with no shaking, then I could hardly begrudge you that.

Because you didn't want my visits, I started to stay away. Dad too. Mum faithfully carried on taking fruit juice to the hospital every day. She might have missed a day or two. Sometimes she was lucky and managed to get as far as your room but usually the nurses turned her away because, they said, the visit was not conducive to the healing process.

'The healing process? Bollocks!' Mum said angrily. 'You're just letting him slip away.'

On the evening of Friday 1st September, I heard from Alex that you'd come to the end of a sleeping cure. I hadn't seen you for nearly three weeks and so I wanted to visit you as soon as possible the next day.

Mum took me in the car and waited for me outside. She gave me a bag filled with nice things to take in with me.

Oddly enough, no one in the ward turned me away. I just walked straight to your room and opened the door.

You were asleep when I came in. I looked at you and I let out a gasp. You'd been getting thinner all the time but now your face seemed to have collapsed completely. Your skin was as grey as ash and your hair was drab and dull and lank. Your lips were cracked and your mouth was gaping open; it looked as though no one had even taken the trouble to brush your teeth. Your hands were raw from smashing against the bars round the bed and I couldn't understand why they hadn't given you a bed without railings at the side.

I looked at you, and I knew straight away that things would never be right again. Then, just as quickly, I shook the thought from me.

'Hullo Maus,' I said softly. My voice woke you up and your body began to shake violently. It was so bad that I gasped out loud again.

'Ho Wukie, asweep.' You brought the words out with difficulty, sounding friendly but reproachful too. That lousy tremor had come back again, thanks to me. But I saw that the Mona Maus smile had gone from your face.

I put the bag beside the bed, together with the envelope that I'd brought, and sat down on the edge. I grasped your wildly flailing arms as tightly as I could and crossed them at the wrists so that I could keep hold of them with one hand. Then, with my other hand, I pushed your tramping feet down on to the mattress. Slowly, the convulsions subsided into a gentle shaking.

'Look, I've brought some apple juice and grape juice,' I said with artificial brightness when you were calmer again.

I took two bottles out of the bag and put them on the bedside table.

You didn't react. You were staring at nothing, your eyes half-closed and red from sleeping. It was as if you were deliberately ignoring me, as if you were hoping that if you didn't see me, then I couldn't see you, either.

'Do you want something to drink?' I held the bottles in front of your face. You were always thirsty. Your body began to jerk again, because a reaction was expected of you.

'Dring,' you said.

'What do you want, apple juice or grape juice?'

'Awwerjew.'

On the bedside table was a tin mug with a spout. A crooked straw was sticking from it. I opened the bottle of apple juice and half-filled the mug. Then I tried to lift your head so that you could drink, but your neck was so stiff that I couldn't manage it.

I put the mug down and looked to see if the head of the bed was adjustable. It was, but as I winched it upwards, you slid down to the foot of the bed and on to the floor, the sheets in a tangle round your thighs. I was so startled that I let the bedhead fall back again. Stupid, stupid, stupid. I winched the bedhead upwards again and fastened it. Then I grabbed you by the armpits and hauled you back into bed.

Once again I tried to help you to drink, but you were shaking so much that apple juice spilled out of the mug and made dark patches on your light blue pyjamas. I dabbed at the juice with a handkerchief, cross with myself for making such a hash of it. And then, when at last I finally got the straw into your mouth, you forgot to drink.

'Suck on the straw, Maus,' I said. Like a robot, you obeyed. After a couple of sips you had to stop to catch your breath. Then some went down the wrong way and you sneezed. I had to duck to avoid a spray of apple juice and then, realising how prissy I was being, I moved even closer to you in my snowy-white trousers. You could slobber all over me as much as you liked.

Because you kept forgetting to suck, I poured small sips of juice into your mouth and managed to get you to empty two mugfuls.

'I've brought you a present,' I said, and got up to fetch the envelope. I took from it the drawing of the tree that you had wanted for your birthday but never got. I held it up in triumph. 'Look!'

You didn't look, so I held it in front of your face. I forced you to look.

'Vewwer nar,' you said lamely and then looked away again.

I bit my lip, knowing at that moment that I'd made a big mistake. I quickly put the drawing on a table at the far side of the room so that you wouldn't have to see it any more. I could just imagine what you must have been thinking. Luke said that I was going to inherit the drawing and now he's giving it to me! Why? Does he think I'm dying and he'll soon be able to inherit the drawing himself?

I was so scared that you might see it that way but it wasn't what I'd meant at all. It was soon after I came into the room that I realised you were slowly dying, but I had decided to give you the drawing long before that. I wanted to do something nice for you, that's all. But why? I was being so stupid. You weren't going to die. I kept telling myself that everything was going to turn out fine. But I decided then and there that I'd never take the drawing back. Never.

I sat down at your side again, and stroked your face and your hair. Slowly your eyes began to close. I could see that you were falling asleep.

'I can't stay very long today,' I whispered. 'Mum's waiting in the car. But I'll come back tomorrow if you'd like me to.' I got to my feet, and your eyes shot open as the mattress sprang back.

'Pee,' you gasped.

I began to pace nervously round the room. 'OK, but what do I have to do?' I snapped. The squeaking bed was suddenly getting on my nerves.

'Tha. Bowwer.'

There was a urine bottle by the wall. I picked it up and pulled back the sheet. I was so shocked by what I saw that I could hardly move: your legs were bandaged up to your groin, and your stomach was nothing but a hollow between the pointed bones of your pelvis. You had grown so thin. I had only seen people as thin as that in pictures of corpses in Nazi concentration camps. I felt like howling at the top of my voice.

I put your willy in the mouth of the bottle, as if it was the most natural thing in the world for me to do. There was just one thought uppermost in my mind: don't spill any!

You peed on command. When you had finished, I pulled the sheet back and disappeared behind a screen to rinse the bottle in the washbasin.

And then, in a perfectly clear voice, you called out, 'Luke, don't go,' and a warm wave of pleasure swept through my entire body. I was so happy that you wanted me to be with you.

'It's OK, I'm staying a bit longer,' I said, and then hurried back to the bed. I crouched down beside you and stroked your cheek with the back of my hand. Your skin felt warm and moist.

Slowly, jerkily, you turned your face towards me as the tremor ebbed away.

'Hi, Lukie.'

'Hi, Maus,' I said softly. I smiled but your face stayed motionless. And then, for one brief moment, you gazed straight into my eyes. You looked at me, and that was the very last time you saw me.

'If I come tomorrow,' I whispered. 'Do you want me to come tomorrow?' No answer. 'If I come tomorrow, then can I bring Mum with me?'

Your eyes closed. You were breathing heavily but you weren't shaking any more. I went on stroking you, running my fingers gently through your hair, across your ear, along your neck.

'I've got to go now,' I whispered, so as not to break the silence. 'See you tomorrow.'

You didn't raise any objection. I eased myself off the bed, bent over you and carefully pressed a kiss on your forehead. You were snoring gently and I saw that you had fallen asleep.

I crept out of the room, closing the door behind me, and then I tiptoed away. Only when I had passed three other rooms did I dare let out a deep breath and run from the hospital.

On Sunday I went back but the sister said that you'd just started a new sleeping cure and so you weren't allowed any visitors. To be perfectly honest, I was relieved that I didn't have to see you.

On Monday you died. When Mum told me, I already knew, but I wanted to hear it out loud. My brother was broken beyond repair. No guarantee. No exchange. No compensation. You were fourteen years and six months old. Less one day.

I was so shocked on that second day of September, the last time I saw you. When I saw what had become of my beautiful little brother, and where all that growing from baby to toddler to boy to teenager had led: to a brother on the verge of death. That image remained on my retina as the only brother I knew to be real. With one stroke all the other things about you that I'd collected in my head, all of them, were no longer true. You weren't the little horror who used to scribble on my drawings. That boy was already dead, as you lay there helpless. You were no longer the collector of old maps. That boy was dead too. You weren't the brother who always wanted to know what I was doing. That boy had gone. And these memories of everyday things no longer seemed to matter when I saw you lying worn out in that bed. They all fell apart. Only one image remained razor-sharp in my otherwise empty head: you dying. Do you understand now why I sometimes prefer to remind myself of you with an old photograph? It doesn't hurt as much.

On Monday you decided not to begin another week. You gave up your life. Or God stole it from you, the dirty thief.

Mum arrived at the hospital at two o'clock in the afternoon. She had only just walked into the ward when the nurses rushed past, pushing you on a trolley to Intensive Care. Mum wanted to follow you but she just couldn't move, she said. She was still standing on the very same spot, clutching her stupid bag of fruit juice, when they came to tell her you were dead. Your brain stem had stopped passing on the message 'Keep breathing'. So you stopped breathing. I don't know if it's the same as suffocating. But I didn't understand any of it anyway, because that wasn't part of the bargain! How can a boy of fourteen, in a psychiatric ward because he had problems with his mind, suddenly die? No one dies just because a doctor says he's not getting enough attention. And yet that's what happened.

You died all on your own. I hope that you didn't know that you were dying. I hope that you were sleeping when it happened and didn't wake up. Or else that you just happened to blink one last time and tripped over your eyelashes.

Maus, when you died no one could explain why. In cases where the cause of death isn't clear, a postmortem examination is performed. This means that your body is opened up after death to try and find out what went wrong.

We knew that one particular doctor had given you a final once-over but we received no information. Mum and Dad phoned Doctor H nearly every day, because he was the leader of the medical team that had treated you. They wanted to find out the results of that last examination; we wanted to know why you had died, because we just couldn't believe that you had died from a lack of attention. As if you had been murdered by your father and mother and brother.

Mum and Dad never got any further than Doctor H's assistant and she always had three excuses at the ready: the doctor hasn't any information yet; the doctor is not available; the doctor is busy with a patient. But they didn't leave it there and continued to bombard the practice with telephone calls. This went on for nearly six months and then an answer came at last.

About ten days ago we received an envelope in the post from Doctor H's assistant. She had sent us the report of the postmortem, just as it was, with no explanation at all, and we had to work it all out for ourselves.

Mum read some of it and then ran to the loo to throw up. This was sufficient reason for Dad not to look at the report at all. I said that I wanted to read the report, come what may. I couldn't care less how sick it made me feel. I just had to do it.

The autopsy report, to give it the official name, paints a sickening final portrait of you, Maus. It describes what you had become after fourteen and a half years of growing and struggling. Not from the outside but on the inside. Your organs are described in cold medical terms, either complete or in sections.

I didn't need to be sick like Mum but a hundred cold shivers ran right through me. I just couldn't understand how such a cold and dry account of a corpse could be sent to parents for whom that body had a name. I won't bore you with the gory details, but every organ that you are supposed to have was present and correct in your body. You may like to know that. So at least you were a complete person when you were alive.

Mum and I took the report to our new family doctor and he explained it all to us. You died from Wilson's disease. This meant that Mum had been right all along when she insisted that you didn't have psychiatric problems but were just plain ill. And I was wrong. I admit it now.

We had never even heard of Wilson's disease and I don't think you had, either, so I'll try and explain it as best I can.

Eating is good for you but not if food were to be pushed straight into your veins, of course. Your body breaks down what you eat into matter that you need, and the rest you pee and crap out. Wilson's disease is a fairly rare metabolic disorder which occurs when your body fails to recognise the metal copper. Just like iron (which you get in spinach, remember), copper is found in food but is something you only need in very small amounts. Instead of getting rid of most of the copper, your system accumulates it in organs which already have a little of it, your brain, for instance, and your liver. Too much copper poisons your organs. It kills them. Not all at once, but little by little. Wherever healthy tissue is touched, a scar develops in the form of connective tissue. You could compare it with the straw stuffing inside a teddy bear.

Because you carried on eating and more and more copper was absorbed into your body, your insides were slowly poisoned with no one being any the wiser. Your organs turned to straw, so to speak. No wonder that everything slowly began to go wrong with you. No wonder you became more and more confused and more and more silent. How could your brain of straw take in any information?

The tremor was caused by your affected brain. And the Mona Maus smile on your face was caused not by some private joke but by the illness. In medical jargon it's called the 'vacuous smile' and it's a typical characteristic of Wilson's disease. I don't know what causes it. Perhaps the part of the brain that gives your facial muscles the signal to smile is the most susceptible to copper. That was the ultimate mockery: dying with a smile on your face.

So there you are, Maus, and not a single doctor discovered it. I read in a book in the library that people with tremors should be tested for the more frequently occurring diseases of which shaking is a characteristic. And that's exactly what happened, even though this type of illness mainly affects people who are older. It also said in the book that in the case of younger patients it should therefore be seen if the illness can be attributed to Wilson's disease. And that's the examination that no one carried out.

'So the psychiatric problems weren't really mental

problems?' Mum asked the doctor, just to make doubly sure.

'No, not in the sense that they had a mental cause. Marius did have psychiatric problems, of course, but they were caused by the physical disorder.'

'But if this disease is so rare,' I said, 'then maybe it's only to be expected that they didn't spot it.'

'The disease isn't as rare as all that. It's just that none of the doctors thought of it. They all looked to see which direction the first doctor had taken and simply followed his lead. And I'm afraid to say that once doctors get an idea in their heads it's very difficult to shift them.'

'So if they *had* discovered it, then Marius would still be alive?'

'No,' said the doctor. 'Marius would have died anyway.'

When we came home, Mum rang Doctor H and actually managed to get him to the telephone! She tore strips off him, very politely of course, and he slammed down the receiver after snapping, 'Even if we had known it was Wilson's, it still wouldn't have made any difference at all. There was nothing that could have been done. Good day to you, madam.'

So you were right, Maus: you weren't crazy. They put you in the wrong ward. Those lousy doctors! They all copied each other, one after the other, and wrote down the wrong answer each time. And there was nothing we could have done to stop it. Mum asked the doctor if there was anything to be gained by lodging a complaint with the

State Inspectorate for Health, because the doctors kept making the wrong diagnosis. But it seems we wouldn't have had a leg to stand on. During your lifetime, the doctors had only made suggestions as to the possible cause of your trouble and had never decided on a diagnosis. And without a diagnosis there can't possibly be any mistake.

But that's not all, Maus. The disease is hereditary. When you were born, your body already knew that you would get Wilson's disease.

Quite by chance, without even realising it, both Mum and Dad were carriers of Wilson's. They didn't get ill themselves because they each only had half the disease in their genes. But together they could pass Wilson's on to their children, who would each have four chances: *one* to get the disease and *three* not to get the disease. You were out of luck.

We were brothers and therefore fairly similar to each other. Exactly the same chances apply to me. I have *one* chance that I've inherited the healthy half of Dad and the healthy half of Mum. In that case, there's nothing to worry about. The other two chances are that I've inherited the diseased half of Dad and the healthy half of Mum, or the healthy half of Dad and the diseased half of Mum. Then I won't get ill myself but I can pass Wilson's on to my children (who must now be really glad that they're never going to be born).

Quite soon, at eleven o'clock this morning to be exact, I've got an appointment with the eye specialist at the hospital, and on Wednesday I've got to see a specialist in internal diseases. They're going to examine me to see if I've got any of the symptoms of Wilson's.

I'm feeling apprehensive, of course, but not as nervous as I thought I would be. There's nothing I can do about it, after all. And I don't want to make it seem better than it is, but if I do get the disease, then at least it will go some way towards rectifying the injustice of an elder son surviving his younger brother. And it would settle, once and for all, the question of whether I am still a brother now that you're dead, because we would then be just two dead brothers.

Don't think for a minute that I'm sitting here hoping to get Wilson's disease, because I definitely don't want to die, not even for you. You do understand that, don't you?

Dad and Mum and I are the only ones who know about this but we don't want to talk about it. It's a sort of taboo. When Mum said that she wanted to burn your things today, I thought at first she was having a clear-out so that she could start mourning me. But I didn't say anything. There wouldn't be any point because Mum would never admit it.

Perhaps I should explain why a visit to the eye specialist is necessary. The disease is quite easy to diagnose by examining the eye (not a single doctor took the trouble to have a really good look at you; did they even bother to ask your name?). Copper accumulates in the eyes and, with the right apparatus, is visible as a green ring.

The other specialist is going to examine my liver on Wednesday. No, he isn't going to cut my body open. Well, not right away, anyhow.

I've just had a sudden thought: what if we are both homosexual because we inherited it from our parents, like our fair hair? Mum and Dad are carriers so they aren't gay themselves (and they haven't got fair hair, either, now I come to think of it) but they can pass it on to their children. That would be a laugh, wouldn't it?

Maus, it's six o'clock in the morning already. A carnival reveller dressed as Dracula has just gone wandering past, leaving a trail of vomit behind him. Probably from guzzling too much blood. And I've just seen next door's cat sneaking across the street. Must get home before it's light, he seems to be thinking, then they won't ask where I've been all night. That goes for me too. So I'll say sleep well, Maus.

Morning

Dear Maus,

I'd set the alarm clock just to be on the safe side but I woke up from a dream after just a couple of hours. It was one of the most beautiful dreams I've ever had and perhaps that's why I'm now feeling so contented, rested and alert.

There was a beautiful island in the sea, an island that was yours and mine, together. The sun was shining. We were standing on the island but we were also the island itself. The island was called Pangaea, I'm pretty sure of that.

All at once something terrible happened, but I wasn't frightened because everything was in slow motion. The island broke in two, right down the middle. We were each left standing on one half, tightly holding hands. But the pieces slowly began to drift apart and I had to let go of you. At that moment you fell gently face down in the sea. I took a flying leap and managed to reach your half of the island. But when I pulled you out of the water by your hair, you had already drowned. But it didn't matter, because we were together and that was the most important thing.

I watched as my half of the island drifted out of sight and disappeared beyond the horizon.

Leisurely, I began to dig a hole and that took all night. When morning came, I looked round and saw a little speck on the horizon that was steadily growing larger. It was my half of the island that had drifted round the globe, just like yours. The two halves collided once again. But the parts that had once been the coast were now inland.

I dragged you into the pit but I didn't cover you with sand. And then I walked back to my side of New Pangaea. End of a beautiful and really peaceful dream. Perhaps because in it the sun and the moon had both been shining so bravely.

At a quarter to nine, when Dad had already been in his office for some time, I went upstairs with a mug of coffee for Mum. I wanted to find out what time she's going to burn your things. I thought that if I left her to sleep, with any luck she won't have time to empty your room and burn everything before I get back from the hospital. But at the same time she might just as easily get up the minute I've gone, and the whole lot could go up in smoke while I'm still in the waiting room. And then there'll be no point in handing her this diary with a dramatic gesture.

'Good morning,' I whispered in her ear. 'Coffee.'

She shot up from her pillow as though she'd been bitten by a snake. Then she opened her eyes sleepily and said, 'Oh God, I've overslept. I've got to take you to the hospital.'

'No, I want to go on my own and I need to get going by half-past-ten.'

Mum sank back on the pillow and turned her back on me.

'Oh yes, that's right. Why did you wake me up, then? I want to snooze a bit longer.'

'What time are you going to burn Marius's things?'

'I don't know. I've got all day. Some time this afternoon, I suppose. And now will you leave me in peace?'

'Mum?'

'No.'

'Don't then.'

'Oh, all right, if you must.'

'I've got a question.'

'What's yellow and dangerous? Shark-infested custard.'

'Mu-um. Can't you just listen to me for a moment?'

'Hmn.'

'After Marius died, you were still a mother. My mother. But I lost my only brother. My question is: am I still someone's brother or have I become an only child?'

'What sort of question is that so early in the morning?' Her head stayed motionless on the pillow. I thought that she wasn't going to give me an answer but after a while there came a sound: 'I think that's something you'll have to decide for yourself.'

'I think that I'll always be a brother but not to anyone who's there.'

'Fine, dear.'

'No, I want to know how you feel about it.'

It looked as though Mum had fallen asleep again but after a moment or two she began to talk. 'They ask me sometimes how many children I've got. Sometimes I say I've got two, sometimes one. And the other day I heard your father say that he's got one child and is another child short.' Mum turned and looked at me with swollen eyes. 'I'm still the mother of Marius, it says so on his birth certificate. And I'm on your birth certificate too, so I presume you're still his brother.' Her hand reached towards the bedside table. I handed her the mug of coffee.

'Even though he doesn't exist any more?'

'I can still remember how Marius didn't want to come out when it was time for him to be born. However hard I strained, that little fellow kept hanging on to my ovaries for dear life. A mother doesn't forget that sort of thing in a hurry.'

'I don't know what you mean.' I squatted down by the bed.

'You're always telling me that my stomach's too fat but it's all your fault that it's like that. You and Marius wore it out when you were growing inside me.'

'Sorry.'

'It's only half your fault,' she said with a sly smile. 'My stomach went nice and firm again after you were born. And then along came Marius and he stretched my stomach a second time. And you can't keep stretching a piece of old knicker elastic for ever, you know.'

'You mean that your stomach is proof that you're the mother of more than one child?'

Mum just looked at me and smiled. I thought that the conversation was over but, just as I was about to get up, she said something else. 'From the seventh month onwards you used to come and take a peep outside because you were in such a hurry to be born.' There was a twinkle in her eyes now. 'Funny, really. I thought that you were going to be a right little tearaway and that Marius would be a timid little bird but it turned out the other way round.'

'I'm not a timid little bird. A dying swan, perhaps.'

Mum gave me a long look and then said, 'You won't remember this but when you were eleven your father and I went on holiday to Switzerland. And I got a letter from you.'

'I've forgotten about that.'

'I can remember that letter word for word.'

I couldn't quite see what this letter had to do with my question but I was curious, even so.

'Dear Mum, Auntie Kees is looking after us very well and I hope that you and Dad are having a nice time in the mountains. For the last few days I have had a terrible stomach ache. Where do you keep the aspirins?'

'I don't remember that at all.'

'Your letter took days to reach us so I rang Auntie Kees to tell her that you had a stomach ache.' She reached out and fondled my ear lobe. 'That's you all over. No one must ever know when you're in pain.'

I said nothing.

'That's why you've always been my little hero,' she said softly. 'You were often sick but you never complained, not like Marius who'd start whining if the sun got in his eyes.'

'That's not true,' I said. 'I never once heard him complain all the time he was ill.'

Mum's face froze. Only her right eyebrow twitched slightly.

'You're quite right,' she said stonily. 'And I always hoped it was because he was never in pain.' She took a sip of coffee and looked about her. 'Now where's the paper? Don't tell me you've forgotten it again?'

I've got to go now, Maus. If the tests don't take too long, I'll still have time to tell you how things went with the eye specialist. I hope that you still want to know.

I'm more scared than I like to admit but I don't want Mum to go with me. If the doctor says that I'm going to die, I want to be able to tell Mum and Dad that there's nothing the matter with me. I think I have the right to do that.

Afternoon

Dear Maus,

When I turned into the street and looked at our house, I fancied I could see a wisp of smoke. Once I got home I raced round the back to see if Mum had lit a fire in the garden. She hadn't even started! She was dragging out boxes of your things and I asked if she needed any help.

She told me that she wanted to do it all by herself, but if I'd like to bring the kitchen chair out into the garden, that would be all right. She didn't ask how it had gone at the hospital.

Before I carried on writing, I took a look inside your room. It is completely bare. Your bed's still there and your desk and chair too. But everything else has gone. Including that lousy drawing. I'll be happy when that goes up in flames.

There are white patches on the wallpaper where maps and posters used to hang. All at once there's a lot more light in the room, or so it seems.

Maus, you know what the plan is and you're still in total agreement, OK? In a little while I'll take our diary down to Mum so that she can burn it. I must keep an eye on how she's doing. That's why I've just been into the spare room to look out of the window. I could see that Mum has still got four boxes full of stuff to go. So I've still got plenty of time left to write.

At two minutes to eleven I reported at the desk in the hospital. I had to wait fifteen minutes, though it seemed more like an hour to me. Then I had to sit behind a large piece of machinery that looked like an instrument of torture.

'I'm going to put some anaesthetic drops in your eye,' the doctor said, as I pressed my forehead against a brace; I wasn't allowed to move my head or blink.

'Why do you have to do that if all you need to do is take a look?' I asked anxiously.

'I've got to put this little thing on the lens of your eye and it would be much too painful without anaesthetic.' She showed me a little tube. It was about the size of a small battery. I didn't want that thing anywhere near my eye but I didn't dare say so.

She took a little bottle and unscrewed the cap. 'Ready?'

'Hmn,' I muttered. One shouldn't make too much of a fuss but at the same time one shouldn't pretend that it's nothing at all.

Cold drops fell in my eye and I fought the urge to blink. I felt the pricking of a thousand tiny needles but I didn't say anything. I held my breath as I saw the machinery moving closer. Then one eye went black. I could feel the thing very clearly on my eye but it didn't hurt. I stared straight ahead because there was no chance of having a good look round with that thing plonked on my eyeball! And then it became clear that the little tube wasn't doing the looking but was just an accessory.

The doctor took a piece of apparatus that was about the size of an ordinary camera and clicked it on to the little tube. I found myself thinking that any minute now the whole caboodle was going to push my eye straight into my brain and then my thoughts would be smashed up for good. But luckily it didn't happen.

It didn't really hurt but it wasn't very pleasant either, and I was getting terribly hot. And why was she taking such a long time? I felt myself start to tremble with nerves and that's why I blurted out something really inane, in the hope that the trembling would go away: 'Well, now that you're taking such a good look, what colour are my eyes exactly?'

The doctor laughed. 'Surely you've looked in a mirror?' she said.

'Yes,' I said. 'I think I've got green eyes but everyone else says they're brown.'

'They're a mosaic of different colours,' she said. 'You've

certainly got a lot of green in your eyes but there are different shades of brown there too, from chocolate to gold.'

Here we go, I thought to myself.

'Is that gold copper?' I asked, hardly moving my lips.

'No, it's just a golden, yellowish colour.'

'But the green, is that the green of those rings?'

'No, no, no, that's just the colour of your eyes.' She straightened up, took the viewer from the accessory and said, 'Nothing to worry about there.' She lifted the accessory from my eye with a little plop. I had to rub my eye because a trace of cold air was left hanging there.

'No green rings?'

'No rings.'

'So I haven't got Wilson's disease?'

'No, not at the present time anyway. But I believe you're having another examination later this week, right?'

I nodded.

'I wouldn't worry about it, if I were you. The chances of you having Wilson's are really very small indeed.'

'But how great is the chance that I might get it in the future?'

'I really can't say.'

At that moment I felt so relieved and yet at the same time guilty all over again. We were brothers and we shared a great secret, so we were more alike than ordinary brothers. But, like a kind of judge, the doctor had passed an interim verdict: 'In the matter of Wilson's disease, I declare that these brothers are not alike.' The parting of brothers. Maus, we're drifting apart from each other like the continents of Pangaea. But you yourself wrote that the separated parts of the world are drifting all the time and will collide with each other again one day. Then a new continent will be formed. Just like the island in my dream. New Pangaea.

'But what help is that?' I asked. 'If I come back next week and I have green rings then, it will mean that I'm going to die after all.'

She looked at me stupidly.

'Whatever gave you that idea?'

'You can't do anything to stop Wilson's.'

'That's completely untrue,' she said with such authority that I began to feel confused.

'It *is* true,' I said. 'Our own doctor and Doctor H both said that my brother would have died whatever happened.'

'Oh, but my boy, you've got it all wrong. It was too late for your brother, but it isn't too late for you. Each time you go to your doctor with the slightest pain, he'll check right away to see whether he's dealing with Wilson's disease. And Wilson's can be kept under control by diet and medication. What those other doctors meant was that the disease had progressed too far in your brother's case for anything to be done about it. You have to nip it in the bud early on. Do you understand?'

I must have looked really upset because she went to

fetch me a glass of water. She meant well, but I didn't need the water and I asked if I could go. She nodded.

I ran straight out of the hospital and went in search of a quiet corner because I needed a really good cry. I felt so terribly sad, because I realised that you would still be alive now if the doctors had discovered in time which disease you had. But those stupid idiots only found out what it was after you were dead. Too late for you, but thanks to you, not too late for me. I know that if I get the same illness, you will have saved me by your example, a sacrifice that should, by rights, be granted by an elder brother to a younger one. There are lots of stories about that. That's how they become heroes. But not me.

I also wanted to howl with rage. I felt so cheated. All because that lousy Doctor H hadn't raised the alarm right away when it became clear which illness you had died from. He did nothing for nearly six months, even though he knew that it was an hereditary disease and that it was only at the outset that anything could be done. That bastard had put my life on the line! He should have rung right away to let us know how important it was that I should be examined. But he kept quiet for six whole months. He'd have let me die, if need be, just to make things look better for him.

I had the wind against me on the way home. Only right and proper, I thought to myself. Thanks to what I'd learned at the hospital, the burden of Wilson's had fallen from my shoulders, but there was still something else that I had to face. Even if it was only the wind against me.

I've just been into the spare room to look out of the window. Mum has lit a small fire right under the cherry tree. She's sitting on the kitchen chair in her winter coat and she's throwing your things on the fire.

It was certainly a beautiful idea. And with any luck I'll be able to play a part in her ritual when I take her this diary. That will be my farewell to you. And time's running out, because she's about to start on the last box.

I'm sorry to say that I haven't managed to get hold of any clear evidence to help me decide whether I'm still a brother or not. Yet at the same time I've found a solution that seems logical to me. By accident.

Last night I wrote, quite by chance: 'When we were both still alive. . .' I wanted to correct this, because you aren't alive any more and I am. But I didn't do it. I left it as it was. It brought back all kinds of memories that I thought I had lost. You came into them, as a boy of ten, thirteen, fourteen. But I came into the memories too, as a boy of eleven, thirteen, fifteen. And they were all of 2nd September last year or before that. After 2nd September I have no memories in which we are brothers. There are no memories in which you are fifteen and I am sixteen. Those brothers don't exist. That is a fact.

Do you realise what this means, Maus? When you died, the brother that I was died also. I told you about the tingling I felt when Mum said that you had died; that must have been the moment when the brother inside me died. But it doesn't end there, because I'm still alive and the memories that I have really do exist. And tonight I had a very clear feeling that some part of you is still alive. We came across each other somewhere. It wasn't in my room, because you weren't there. And it wasn't at your grave or in heaven, because I wasn't there. But it doesn't really matter where it was. It could have been that we met each other halfway across New Pangaea, the beautiful island that is ours alone, because no one knows where it lies.

More important still: something of you is still alive and I think I know how this is possible. If it is true that the brother in me died with you, then it is equally true that the brother in you survived with me! And this seems so logical, for where else would the brother in you remain? That brother in you – is me.

I am that brother still, and this will go on and on and on, my whole life long. And I don't need this diary for that. You've been reading it over my shoulder all this time anyway.

Goodbye, dear Maus. A kiss from

Your brother

Evening

Dear Maus,

I've already said goodbye, but I'm back with some news: this diary won't be going up to you in smoke. Let me tell you how it all came about.

At the very last minute I went downstairs to take this diary to Mum. I noticed that the door to the office was open and so I peered inside. Dad was watching Mum, on the quiet, through a gap in the net curtains.

'Why don't you take the other chair from the kitchen and go and sit with her?' I suggested. 'Then you can do it together.'

'No, no, no, it's for your mother to do on her own,' Dad said. 'I can follow it all from here. How did you get on at the hospital, my boy?'

I went and stood beside him and said, 'I haven't got Wilson's.'

'We didn't think you had. But I'm relieved just the same.'

'Me too. Dad, there's something that isn't very clear to me. Is Wilson's a terminal illness or not?' I wanted to know if I was the only one who had got the wrong idea.

'There's no possible cure as far as I'm aware.'

My first impulse was to tell him what the doctor had said to me but I didn't, because Dad would then realise that there had been no need for you to die. And what would be the point of that? It wouldn't bring you back again. It would just be yet more bad news. But if *I* got the disease, then it would make sense to say that you don't need to die from Wilson's because it becomes good news right away then.

'I'm going to tell Mum that everything's OK with me,' I said.

'Must you do that *now*?' Dad asked. He straightened his tie and put a hand on my shoulder. 'Yes, of course you must tell her the good news. But don't say that I'm watching. Your mother doesn't need to know that.'

I turned to go out of the study. Then I saw the drawing hanging on the wall, the drawing that I gave to you. I was just about to say something when I thought better of it and went away in silence. If Dad liked the drawing that much, then he deserved to keep it. You don't mind, do you?

I walked into the garden and went straight up to Mum. She was halfway through the last box and looked annoyed when she saw me approach.

'I want to be left on my own,' she said irritably. 'Why can't you get that into your head?'

'Haven't you forgotten Marius's diary?' I said.

'And I suppose you've come riding gallantly to the rescue like a proper little Don Quixote?'

'No, like a dying swan.' I offered Mum the diary and said rather pompously, 'Here you are then. Throw it on the fire.'

Mum didn't move. I thrust the diary at her.

'Go on, take it.'

'I'm not going to burn that diary,' she said.

I didn't understand what she meant. I stared at her, wide-eyed.

'I never had any intention of burning his diary,' she said without taking her eyes from the flames. 'You just jumped to conclusions as usual. If you'd only taken the trouble to ask me what I was planning, but no.' One by one she dropped into the fire the wooden sandals that Auntie Kees had given you. 'Now just go away and leave me alone, there's a good boy.'

'But you said that you were going to throw absolutely everything in the fire.'

'In a manner of speaking, darling, in a manner of speaking. I'm not going to burn books, am I? No one does that any more, not since Hitler.'

I stood there, open-mouthed. In one single moment she had snatched away my part in the ritual. I felt anger rising inside me and I thought: I'll throw the diary in the flames myself! But I didn't. I couldn't. To be responsible for burning your thoughts was one step too far for me. Which meant that the wind had been taken out of my sails.

It was to have been a really great moment, handing over our diary to Mum. She would have burned it and I'd have been free of guilt at last. Beautifully planned. But Mum didn't do as I expected and I didn't dare destroy your diary myself. I felt like a coward and I definitely didn't want to be that.

There and then, in one second flat, I came to an important decision. I could feel my knees start to buckle and the nerves screaming in my throat. I really didn't have the courage, but I forced myself. Mum's ritual couldn't proceed unless I contributed something really important. My own ritual, mine alone, much bigger than anything that Mum could imagine. And in a flash I knew exactly how to introduce it. I said, 'Don't you want to know how things went at the hospital?' I could hear my voice trembling. Mum didn't respond so I pressed on.

'You always used to say that however bad things may seem, they could always be even worse and so they're never really as bad as all that. I've got bad news but luckily I've got some good news as well.' My heart was pounding as if it was trying to burst out of my body. 'The good news is that I don't have Wilson's. . .' I took a deep breath before going on with my sentence.

'I know that already,' said Mum, and a map of Europe went up in flames. 'You surely don't think that I'd just sit here waiting? I rang the hospital ages ago.'

It was as if I'd been given a slap in the face.

'Surely you could have waited!' I shouted. 'I wanted to tell you myself.'

'Yes, I know, so you can kid me that you're blind in your left eye and have got a cataract in the right eye and can't go to school for a fortnight.'

I told myself not to respond, even though I felt like hitting her. As if I'd invent rubbish like that about something so important. She didn't trust me and she wanted to get even with me. But I had to press on, it was now or never, and once again I began one of the most important sentences I've ever spoken in my life. 'I've got good news and I've got bad news. The good news is that I don't have Wilson's disease and so I'm going to stay alive. And the bad news is. . . that I don't fancy girls, I prefer boys.'

It had been said. I had said it and it could be heard. And now for the fall-out. I looked up at the sky to see if a hurricane was approaching or if there was a message of some sort – the occasion surely demanded a message from you from on high. Clouds were drifting slowly overhead and I suddenly had the feeling that you were waving at me.

Mum said nothing and stared into the fire. And then she gave a sigh.

'I can't say that I like it,' she said rather flatly, 'and I wish that things were different, but it doesn't come like a bolt from the blue.'

'What do you mean?' I asked in amazement. 'Don't you understand what I'm saying? I'm one of *those*.'

'I heard you the first time,' said Mum. She raked the flames with the poker from the fireplace. 'We'd be pretty poor parents if we didn't know our own son just a little bit.' She gave the deepest sigh that I've ever heard in my life. 'Just as long as you're happy, my boy. That's the most important thing.'

I was seething with emotion as never before. I was angry, happy, bashful, grateful, cheeky, and delirious with joy. The hurricane that I'd expected hadn't come from above but was raging inside me instead. I said, 'But I'm not happy at all. The point is that I can never make *you* happy now.'

'There's no need to worry about us,' said Mum. 'You mustn't feel any responsibility for the happiness of your father and me. Just make sure that you're happy yourself.'

'But you don't understand!' I cried. 'You'll never have any grandchildren, thanks to me!'

'Then we'll get a dog,' Mum said curtly. 'Or a cat, if your father prefers.' She prodded the flames once again and then looked at me. 'You can hope to have grandchildren but you have no right to them.'

I didn't know whether I was coming or going. My brain was turning cartwheels in my skull and I could feel pain rising deep within my head.

'So you knew all the time that I wasn't happy and you also knew why!' I said angrily. 'And yet you still let me muddle on even though there was no need for it.'

'Now then, calm down,' Mum pleaded. 'We didn't know for certain. And as long as we didn't talk about it, nothing was definite. It could have gone either way.' Then, more to herself than to me, she added, 'You're still so young.'

'But if you'd only once, just *once*, even in a very general way, just casually, let me know that it even *existed*! That it had a name even. Surely you could have let me know that I wasn't the only one in the world?' I had to bite my lower lip to stop it trembling.

'Well, I won't lie to you,' said Mum. 'Naturally your father and I hoped that you'd be heterosexual. And, as things have turned out, perhaps it would have been more sensible if we'd said something about it. . .' She left her sentence unfinished and threw your bookends in the fire. 'Will you leave me alone now? We'll talk about it tonight, when Dad is here.'

I turned round and saw Dad behind the net curtains. The world was spinning and my throat felt dry and tight because I had dared to tell my secret. And the only response I'd got was that it hadn't come like a bolt from the blue.

'So you just thought I'd get over it?' I shouted, allowing my lips to quiver now. 'That's sheer child abuse! I kept quiet about it all this time just for your sake, because I thought I'd make you unhappy. And yet you let me carry on suffering on purpose.'

'Do stop making such a fool of yourself, please!'

Mum said. 'No mother or father would ever encourage homosexuality. They'd be crazy if they did. No one wants to condemn their child to a life of discrimination and bullying. That's not what you want for your child.'

'But surely you knew I was being bullied? That's what you wanted for me, was it?'

'Luke, we'll talk about it this evening.'

'And now that nothing's changed, you suddenly expect me to be happy, do you? Just like that, I suppose?'

'You've only just turned sixteen, remember,' Mum said scornfully, 'but if you really know for certain that you're gay then I'll resign myself to it. So find yourself a friend, or bring him home if you already have one. I won't be difficult about it. Boyfriend or girlfriend, whoever it is will still be a tart who isn't good enough for my son.'

'Yes, very funny, Mum.'

'I could go off and have a really good cry if you like, but I can't change anything, can I?'

'And Dad?' I took another look at the window where he was standing without being able to hear a word we said.

'Your father realised much sooner than I did. He had his suspicions when you were only three.'

'Why didn't either of you help me just a little bit?' I asked quietly, digging my nails hard into the palms of my hands until the pain seemed an echo of the pain in my head. 'Suddenly you're saying that it's important for me to be happy but when I wasn't and you knew perfectly well why, you didn't give a damn. And all because you'd much rather have had a child who was straight.'

'You've made your point, Luke. You're beginning to repeat yourself. I don't want to talk about it any more. There's plenty of time for that. I want to be alone with my thoughts of Marius now. Just leave me in peace for a little while, please.'

My knees were shaking with tension and I didn't know what more to say. I didn't know what I should be feeling because I was so upset. I couldn't become a hero by sacrificing this diary but neither could I be a hero by giving up my secret. Because Mum and Dad had known all along and kept it secret from me most of my life. And all that time they had deliberately left me in the lurch. Why? Because a child who is gay can only be granted happiness if he is *really* sure he isn't straight. As if he has a choice in the matter.

I turned and legged it indoors. I flew up the stairs and paced up and down my room. I tried to calm myself down and gather my thoughts but it wasn't as easy as that to clear a path through my head. I felt weighed down by the thought that all my life I had been prepared to be unhappy because I thought this would cause the least unhappiness for Mum and Dad. And now it turned out that if I'd gone around shouting that I was special from the very beginning, they'd just have said, 'Oh, we've known that all along.'

But one thing slowly became very clear to me. The more I thought about it, the more I realised that Mum had accepted me the way I am without any clauses or conditions, and that is really quite extraordinary. She didn't try to talk me round. She didn't cry to show me how unhappy I'd made her. And she didn't threaten to stop loving me. She didn't kick me out of the house or lock me up in the cellar but just remained my mother. My own mother. She simply accepted it and moved on to other things. I suppose you could say that she values me for what I am. And it seems to me that this is the first time, the very first time it has happened in my entire life!

My secret is a secret no longer. Looking back, I can hardly believe that I dared to do it but I felt that I just had to. Don't you see, Maus, my grand gesture was going to be surrendering our diary, but when that seemed impossible there was only one thing left that I could do. If the diary with my secret inside could not be destroyed, then the secret itself had to be destroyed. And that's what I've done. Whew!

Slowly I began to feel in a mood to celebrate. As if I'd won a prize or a medal and couldn't really believe what was happening to me. Perhaps this was what being happy felt like. I had a sudden urge to punch my fists in the air, to shout we-are-the-champions. I felt so proud of myself and of what I am and what I'd dared to do. I felt like doing something really crazy. The crazier the better.

Just over ten minutes later I walked into the garden with a shopping bag. Mum's boxes were empty now and she was staring at the smouldering heap. I put the bag down, and then took the cake from it that I'd collected from the baker's on the corner, together with twelve plates.

I pretended not to see Mum but I'd already noticed the look of amazement on her face. I tipped the bag upside-down and all the silver cutlery clattered on to the earth beneath the cherry tree.

'What on earth are you doing?' Mum squawked when she saw me daintily laying places on the ground around her fire, the forks to the left and the knives to the right. The preparations for a grand dinner party.

'What does it look like?' I said. 'It's Marius's birthday and you forgot to buy a cake.'

'How can you be so stupid! You're the one who'll have to clean the silver if it gets dirty.'

'Fine,' I said, and I cut the cake into twelve pieces which I put on to the twelve plates.

'Would you like a slice of cake?' I asked.

'No, I'm on a diet, as well you know.'

'Don't then.'

Mum stood and watched, a little undecided, her arms

on her hips. Then she shrugged and said carelessly, 'You go ahead then, my boy. But just remember to clear everything away, as well as the ashes and the chair and the empty boxes. And it's high time some hoeing was done in this garden. And while you're about it, mow the grass as well. All right?'

'Yes,' I said curtly.

I heard her mutter, 'The boy's an imbecile!' but it didn't worry me in the least. She turned and walked to the French windows.

Like an idiot, I started to empty all the plates one by one, each time moving the chair one place on round the smouldering fire. The idea was to have a piece of cake for you and a piece for me, a piece for an Indian who didn't come, for a gypsy who stayed away, for Dad and Mum and Gran, for Alex. For everyone who sometimes thinks of you. But after three pieces of cake, I already knew that I'd be sick all the next day, so I started to take just one tiny mouthful, like Snow White eating from the plates of the seven dwarfs.

Suddenly, Dad stormed outside with the other kitchen chair in one hand and our Mum in the other.

'Is there any cake left?' he asked.

'There's enough,' I said.

Dad sat down on the chair he'd brought and I jumped to my feet as he pushed Mum on to mine.

'Oh all right, then,' she said. 'Just a small piece. As long as I don't have to sing For He's a Jolly Good Fellow.'

Dad didn't want her to do that and neither did I. He did want to know why I'd thrown the beautifully polished silver on the ground, but he waited until his plate was empty before asking.

'When Marius died,' I said, 'I forgot to go and swap him for the silver cutlery.'

'Oh,' said Dad and Mum. And I was glad to see that neither of them had the faintest idea what I was talking about.

Maus, I've washed the plates, cleared away the ashes and taken the chairs back into the kitchen. I've folded the boxes and put them in the dustbin. I've mowed the lawn and raked the earth. And now I'm going to stop writing. I must go. It's high time. I've still got to polish the silver and after that I want to go into town and see if anyone at the carnival recognises me disguised in my own clothes. And then ordinary life will carry on. There'll be French first period, just as always, and theorems in the third. So I'll say goodbye, Maus. Goodbye, goodbye. Will you take good care of the brothers that we were? And I'll look after the brothers that we are.

Cheers,

Luke